50

SPIRALING

BEYOND

OBLIVION

Amy Sutphin

A Twisted Realm Novella

To my husband
My Love

Chapter One

"You're leaving?"

"Yes, we must."

"Why?"

The loud indignant cry rang in Emya's groggy head.

"I can't tell you," Felix said in a calm, level voice, though with a hint of irritation.

"Oh, you and your secret magic. Will you tell me what you're doing after you get Emya killed?"

"Yes," Felix said, his voice now dripping with annoyance. "When she and I are both dead I'll be happy to tell you what's going on."

"I didn't say if you were dead."

Spurred by the imminent fight, Emya sat up and looked around. Evris sat at the foot of the bed, the sheets balled into her fists, face red with fury staring down at the nervous but resolute master mage who was leaning against the wall across from her.

"What's the matter?" Emya mumbled blearily. Evris looked around guiltily. Felix crossed his arms and looked at the floor, composing himself.

"Sorry, Emya. Felix wanted to wake you up. I was trying to stop him, but I guess I woke you up anyway."

"S'all right," Emya said and yawned. "What does he need me for?"

"We have to get going," Felix said firmly.

"Do you though?" Evris said sardonically. "Do you really?"

"Yes," Emya said, her sleepiness banished immediately by the recollection of the decisions made the night before. Immediately, her friend's face fell in betrayal.

"Are you sure Emya? It could be dangerous. Look what happened last night," Evris said, throwing her arms up dramatically.

"I know," Emya said, keeping her voice steady and resolute, despite the emotion welling up inside her. She didn't want Evris to be upset and she dearly wanted to stay with her friend. However, until she and Felix were free from the Companion, Evris would be in danger. "That's why we have to go. I'm sorry but I can't say any more."

Evris looked from Emya to Felix, then huffed in

defeat.

"I suppose I can't stop you anyway. How long will you be gone?"

"I don't know," Felix said. "Probably a while."

"Well, at least this will give me a chance to catch up to Emya in my magic studies."

Emya smiled consolingly, but then Felix said, "We're going to Asulashio, a city built using some extraordinary constructive magic and home to the world's most extensive library of magic. I intend for Emya to spend a lot of time studying magic."

Evris's mouth fell open in comical disbelief. "Well, that makes me feel better about this Felix."

Felix's mouth also fell open in surprised, speechless embarrassment.

"And I'm sure I still won't learn anything, so you have nothing to worry about Evris," Emya said before giving Evris a consoling hug.

With the most difficult goodbye mercifully over with fewer tears and arguments than Emya had been dreading, the rest of the preparation for their departure went swiftly.

Emya dressed in traveling clothes brought to her by one of the mages, though they were not at all like traveling clothes. A long white skirt and white shirt with long sleeves and loose, lace cuffs. Over that went a pale blue silk dress, the long sleeves flaring out to display the white lace beneath and the skirt parted in the middle so the white beneath peeked out as she walked. It won't last a day's trek down the mountain, she thought as she smoothed the skirt so it lay properly. Neither would the boots of white linen. They wouldn't be white for long.

Puzzling over the strange outfit, she wandered out into the main room where Felix and Evris were waiting. Felix was also wearing clothes unsuitable for the dirt and wet of the mountain. His shirt was dark green and loose like hers, though his sleeves didn't flare out as much. His black pants looked normal and were tucked into polished black boots. He was also wearing a cloak that she recognized as the one given to him by Mr. and Mrs. Mellia. He had an identical one in his hands, which she knew was for her.

"Goodness," Evris said jealously. "You don't look like you're going traveling. You look like you're going to a party."

"I know," Emya said. "This dress won't last one day on the mountain, and look at these boots." She stuck out her foot. "They won't last five minutes before they're completely black."

Felix laughed. "Sorry. I should have explained. We're not going down the mountain."

"We're not?"

"Nope." He shook his head emphatically. Evris squealed in delight. Emya, feeling slow, looked at Felix in confusion.

"You want to tell her, Evris?" he said with a pleased

grin.

"You're going to go by magic!" she burst out, punctuated by another squeal. "I am so jealous. You'll have to tell me all about it when you get back. I want to know what it feels like."

"You don't have to wait until we get back," Felix said. "She's already traveled by magic."

"You have?" Evris said, her eyes wide in awe. "And you never told me?"

"It didn't come up," Emya said, who hadn't wanted to talk about anything magic until she had been at Civim for a while. Then she'd forgotten about it.

"What does it feel like then?" Evris asked, still awestruck.

"Well, we'd better get going. Don't want to keep Kyn waiting for our send-off," Felix said.

"Hey, no fair!" Evris cried as Felix took Emya by the arm and led her to the door.

"She can tell you on the way Evris. Come on."

Emya filled her in on the walk through the rings, and by the time they had arrived in the first ring and headed towards the bridge, the girl was practically glowing with envy.

Emya thought that Felix must have been pulling some sort of prank on them as they crossed. Why were they heading for the mountain if they were traveling by magic? It soon became clear, as they approached the towering arch where the five masters and mistresses stood waiting, that there was more to the strange construct than mere decoration. Artyem greeted them as they arrived. He was wearing the formal uniform of the guards she'd seen stationed in Civim. She'd never seen him wear it before.

"No time for reconsideration speeches," Felix said as he stepped through the group and took two rucksacks from Artyem. As he handed Emya hers, she realized it was the one she had received from Evris's village.

"I wasn't going to attempt one, although there is plenty of time if I was," Master Kyn said. "Especially as you will be needing us if you want to go."

"True," Felix said. "What about you Tyem? You want to try your hand at convincing me not to go?"

Artyem shook his head. "It is not the trip to Asulashio I object to."

Felix laughed. "I'll take that as a victory."

"Enjoy it," Artyem said. "Probably won't happen again."

While they talked, Mistress Tunin hugged Emya and then pushed her into Mistress Hanna's arms.

"Don't be afraid. Just listen to Felix and Artyem and come back to us soon," Hanna said encouragingly. Emya, surprised but pleased by the affection, hugged her back lightly.

"I'll do my best," she said, making no promise about listening to Felix. Though he was clever and driven, Artyem had a clearer head, especially when it came to keeping his charges safe.

"I know you will," Hanna said, releasing her.

Emya followed Felix to the arch where Artyem already stood. Master Kyn positioned them so they were directly underneath it.

Evris, Emya saw, was shuffled behind the Masters though she waved to Emya from between them. Emya waved back and then there was a surge of tingling all over her and the air crackled high above her. She looked up just in time to see a sheet of white rush down from the arch. For several seconds they were covered in the blinding white. And then no longer were they standing under the arch, and the Masters had disappeared.

~~*~*~*~*

Towering over them was an enormous castle made of sandy-colored stone that looked almost like gold, with bits that glittered in the sun. A long, stone bridge spanned a vast moat with steep banks of lush grass on both sides. In both directions, ramparts stretched as far as Emya could see. Far above them, guards patrolled or stood on watch.

Emya followed Felix and Artyem across the drawbridge, glancing over the edge of it to see the foaming, water gushing through a ravine of the same sandy, golden stone. The castle must have been built on a natural ravine. As they approached an outer building

Artyem said was a guardhouse, two guards emerged and waited for them. Their armor was made of leather and polished metal plates.

Artyem spoke to them in their language, and they stepped away. As they passed, Emya tried to look at one of them without gawking, but when the guard caught her gaze, he bowed. A little shocked by the gesture, Emya hurried to the safety of Felix's side. She had no idea how she was supposed to respond. Bow back? Thank him? What she really wanted to know was why he thought he had to bow to her.

A metal gate barred the entrance. Beyond, Emya could see a courtyard of grass and carefully tended shrubs and flowers, like a small slice of the garden in Civim. One of the guards shouted. Chains clinked, metal scraped against metal, and the large gate lifted as they approached. Indeed, there was a small courtyard surrounded by a vast, bustling traffic hub. Emya counted five ornate carriages, each with a team of matching black, white, or chestnut horses. Ladies and lords, dressed in more elaborate and bejeweled versions of the clothes Emya and Felix were wearing, climbed in and out of the carriages that sped off around the square and disappeared into tunnels in the walls. All of this action was directed by haughty men dressed in uniforms of midnight blue with gold braiding along with the cuffs and hem of their tunics.

One of these men approached them. Felix spoke to

him, giving him their names, and presumably explaining who they were. The man must have been impressed because his condescending expression turned to one of utmost reverence and fervor. He bowed deeply then barked orders at another man and they both hurried off.

"What's going on?" Emya asked. She'd been so enraptured since their arrival that she hadn't had time to organize her thoughts.

"They're going to get us a carriage," Felix said. "I know you have questions, but wait until we're safely alone. Most people won't know who we are and it's better that they don't."

"Until word gets out," said Artyem, "then they'll all claim to have seen us in the Edil Courtyard."

"Edil was one of their most renowned kings," Felix informed Emya. "This is the castle's largest courtyard and it connects to all the main roads within the castle walls."

"I didn't know castles could be this big," Emya said. "I've only heard about a few that are a great distance from my village. Some traveled there, and from what they said they were smaller than my village."

Felix nodded. "The Great Plateau doesn't have enough resources to support a large settlement. Most settlements there are like your village. This kingdom, though, is built on land rich in precious metals, jewels, and other ore. It borders the coast, so they can easily export and import goods, and the soil is very fertile."

"The only thing it can't buy is a mage guild," Artyem said with a hint of irony.

"True," Felix said.

Emya had never heard of a mage guild, but she withheld the question as Felix had requested.

After a short while a large carriage, decorated in gold and silver, pulled to a stop. One of the liveried men, no haughtiness visible, helped Emya up the narrow steps. She sat down on a soft bench strewn with delicate lace pillows. She put one on her lap to hold as she didn't want it thrown around her. Though as the carriage gently pulled away, none of the other pillows moved.

"What do you mean by a mage guild?" asked Emya as they seemed to be alone now.

"Some kingdoms have guilds where mages from around the world—but mostly Civim— live, work, and use their magic to make the kingdom better. Unfortunately, some kingdoms thought they could use those mages to fight wars and conquer other lands," Felix explained.

"Mages aren't supposed to do that though," Emya said, remembering her lessons from Master Nikola.

"No, they aren't. But one of their kings thought he could get away with it before Civim took notice. He found a record of an object created to control the will of mages without their noticing. The king sent some powerful mages off to conquer and kill and they didn't realize what they were doing. It took a long time to sort it all out and discover it was the king controlling the mages. In the end, Civim decided that Asulashio would no longer be allowed to have a mage guild and that magical help could only be granted by appealing to Civim. Then we would decide how to proceed."

"So no mages live here?"

"Oh, they do. We've had many students come from this kingdom and many returned here to work on the magical upkeep required for some of the enchantments that have been part of the kingdom for centuries, but there are strict rules about what magic they can do, and they are closely monitored by Civim to make sure they aren't being influenced by any of the nobility or royalty."

"So the nobility and royalty will resent us?" Emya worried aloud.

"Not at all," Felix said. "They will be exceedingly courteous you'll find. The ruling family, unrelated to said king, has been in the good graces of Civim for several generations and is hoping to get the sanctions lifted. The crown prince, in particular, took a big step several years ago and came to Civim to speak with Master Kyn about it. No other monarch had before. He's quite ambitious. He has plans for the good of the kingdom and he knows the only way to implement them requires a mage guild."

"And he's willing to do whatever it takes?" Emya asked skeptically.

"No, he wants to do it right," Felix said. "He has many ideas and plans to make sure the mage guild will be safeguarded from the ambitions of rulers to come."

"Sounds like you admire him," Emya said.

"I do, and I think you will too."

That remained to be seen, but Felix's endorsement was enough to keep her from imagining the worst of the unknown prince.

"I didn't know the Arch could do that," Emya said, changing the subject. "Is it a magic object too?"

"That's what I thought you'd ask," Felix said. "It's not a magic object, exactly. It was made from a rock with magical properties and those natural properties were directed by mages to increase their power, for transportation specifically."

"Sounds like a magical object to me."

"It's not. It's different, not even like the coins, but you won't understand it fully for some time."

"Consider it this way," Artyem said, "it's a magical object, but it was not enchanted by a mage nor can it act on its own accord."

That made sense. The Companion was created by mages and seemed to act on its own accord from time to time. But a naturally magical substance that could be guided and directed by mages, that *was* different.

Emya watched through the window as they drove through tunnels and along a stream that flowed from the river moat. Through a particularly large tunnel, they emerged into a vast garden. Barely visible in the distance were the enormous walls, patrolled by shining dots. Flower beds, and shrubs, skillfully trimmed accented charming water features to please the eyes of the ornamental courtiers that roamed the garden paths, chatting and laughing together as the carriage passed through.

It was like a fairytale. She knew places like this existed. Her mother talked about other lands, but always in a way that made them sound unreal, almost unimaginable. A strange kind of dizziness overcame her as she was struck by how different her life was now.

"Are you alright?" Felix said. He must have sensed her mood.

"Just in awe. I never thought I'd come to a place like this. I don't think I could have imagined it existed."

"It's not that different from Civim," Felix said.

"Not to us," Artyem interjected. "But she's not used to places like this."

"Where is this anyway?" she asked. They had studied some maps in Master Nikola's class, so she had a better idea of where things were relative to the places she'd been, but she didn't recall seeing Asulashio on any map.

"We're on the other side of the world," Felix said. "It would take a year to travel here by conventional methods."

The carriage rattled and creaked to a stop and the door opened, held by one of the simpering servants. Emya followed Felix and Artyem, stepping out into a small courtyard. Sandy yellow stone pillars enclosed matching walkways through gold, orange, and red flowers. Amidst them stood a tall, tan, golden-haired man in his late twenties. He wore scarlet and midnight blue, a dark blue gem pierced through one ear, and a gold chain with an ornate pendant which must have been some sort of crest.

"Welcome," he said in a light, melodically-accented voice. He had no trouble with their language. "I was very pleased to hear of your coming this morning. Though if you'd given me more notice, I could have made better arrangements."

He stepped forward and shook Felix's hand. Emya looked around in surprise. She had not realized that the sun was setting, not rising. How strange to suddenly be in the evening once more. She would not be able to sleep a wink. Though if they were to be going to bed soon after they arrived, Felix could have made her stay up the night before.

"You can drop the false modesty. I know you always have the best for us when we visit, no matter how little notice," Felix said.

The man smiled slyly. "Using your magic to see through my ploy again?"

"Nope, just previous and consistent observation." Felix turned and gestured to Emya. "May I present Emya Messam, a promising new student at Civim and my good friend." Emya's eyes went wide, and her cheeks burned as the man, taking her offered hand, bowed low and kissed it.

"Exceedingly pleased to meet you. It's not often I am introduced to friends of Felix. I didn't know they could be so pretty."

"To be fair, the only other one you've met is me, so that's not saying much," Artyem said flatly. The man, still holding Emya's hand, straightened up.

"Hence, why I didn't know," he said, not taking his hypnotic gaze from Emya. Up close he was quite striking, with full red lips, long black lashes, and piercing blue eyes.

"Emya," Felix said with a gentle nudge to rouse her senses, "this is Prince Othilrin, heir to the throne of Asulashio."

Frozen with indecision, gaping up at the grinning prince still holding her hand, she looked at Felix.

"What am I to do?" she asked. "Bow?"

The prince laughed, low and musical.

"You don't have to do anything," he said. "In this land, you are held in much higher regard than I."

"But, you're a prince. You're going to be king."

"Yes, and when I am then you must 'bow.'" He made a gesture, curling two fingers quickly. Emya didn't know what it meant but understood that it was more complicated than that. All of this was far too much for her to accept. Not a year ago she was the lowest-regarded person in a tiny, no-account village, and now she was told she had a higher station than a crown prince on the other side of the world? No, it was far, far too much to take in. However, if it meant she didn't have to learn to bow, curtsy, or anything else, well then she wouldn't worry about it.

The prince turned and motioned them towards a set of fine, honey-colored wooden doors. He offered his arm to Emya and hesitantly she took it. Felix walked along her other side, while Artyem was close behind. Emya glanced back at him as his gaze shifted from the scenery to her. When their eyes met, he gave her an encouraging smile.

"I can guess the reason for your visit," the prince said to Felix. "You're here to usurp my crown."

"How did you know?"

A liveried servant held the doors open and the four passed through, unaccompanied by the many servants outside. Emya had thought they were there to serve the prince and hadn't liked the idea of a vast entourage of prim servants, but perhaps they had other duties and the prince's presence had suspended them. As they turned down a corridor with high, glass windows to the courtyard, her suspicion was confirmed as the servants had begun sweeping the walkway and scrubbing pillars, walls, and windows.

"Ah, well. The crown is not mine just yet, so you'll have to bring that up with my father."

"No, I respect your father too much, and it would

be too difficult to usurp him," Felix replied with a smile.

"Implying that it would be easy to usurp me?"

"Always."

The prince gave a mock exasperated sigh. "Why I bother with you I'll never know. Now, failing your initial goal, all I was told was that you needed to use the library. Would that be the Great Library? Or the Uires Scriptus?"

"The Scriptus, unfortunately."

The prince blanched. "I thought so, though I'd hoped otherwise. I had the caretakers prepare the scrolls for you just in case."

"Thank you. I know they take some time to set out."

"It's no trouble, though if they weren't so delicate it might not take so long."

"Indeed," Felix said. There was an undertone in the conversation Emya couldn't fathom the meaning of, though she was able to pick up on the twinge of tension. She chanced a look back at Artyem, who shook his head slightly.

As they made their way deeper into the beautiful halls, Emya lost track of the conversation, too enamored by the stunning decoration. Intricate mosaics of ceramic and glass paneled the walls, and soft carpet that matched the predominant color of the mosaics in each hall and chamber crushed delicately under each step. Long drapes of velvet framed the windows. One alcove had an indoor grotto with water tumbling down a mosaic of a mountainside and into a rock pool surrounded by potted plants. Several courtiers sat on the rock, throwing fish food into the pool.

Up they went to a set of wide, carved stone stairs to a set of gilded double doors. Servants stood by, poised to open them.

"This will be Emya's first visit to a castle library," Felix said.

"Indeed?" said the prince, raising his brow at her. "Visit no other after this, or you're sure to be disappointed."

Emya was about to say this was her first visit to a castle as well and that she had no expectations at all when the servant pulled the door open and the words caught in her throat. Towers of spiraling bookcases extended up to several stories, each filled with too many beautifully bound books to count.

"You can't find the books you need in here?" Emya asked as they walked through the spires of books.

"No, unfortunately not. The books I need to consult contain dangerous information and are kept in a protected vault."

"You may peruse the library any time if you wish," the prince said. "It's open to all who desire to learn."

And indeed it was. They passed several servants sitting in cushioned chairs or tables who stood up and bowed or curtsied to the prince before sitting and taking up their books once again.

"The servants are allowed to read in here?" she asked.

"When they're off duty. Though most the people here now are citizens of the city, or they came here from somewhere else in the world, as you did."

Much to Emya's disappointment, her small group exited the library through a simple, unassuming side door into a bare chamber made with the same kind of stone as Civim. In the center of the room, on an old, battered wooden table of some dark hardwood were three long, yellowed scrolls that had been rolled out and secured with small metal figures of a hooded and cloaked person on each corner of the scroll.

Felix stood before the scrolls and sighed deeply. "This is going to take a while."

"I shall leave you to it then," said the prince, "as I am not supposed to be in here at all."

Before departing, he once again took Emya's hand and kissed it, sending her heart fluttering and her head spinning. Then he clapped Artyem on the shoulder and sauntered out, his fine boots making almost no sound on the stone floor.

"I should go—" Artyem started to say before Felix cut him off.

"No."

"I don't think you need me," Artyem protested.

"You're a guard of Civim, it's your duty to keep watch over the mages who live there."

19

Emya looked from Felix's annoyed expression to Artyem's, which was somber and edgy. She knew he did not like magic, but something about the room, or maybe the scrolls, was putting him more on edge than she'd ever seen him before.

After a brief, heated glaring match, Felix looked down at the scrolls again, frowning.

"This is going to take some time," he said. "Perhaps Emya would like to see more of the castle?"

"I shall accompany her."

"Very well," Felix said, then added teasingly, "Emya might like to run into the prince again."

Face burning red hot, Emya turned and hurried back out of the room, Artyem on her heels, leaving Felix chuckling with barely contained mirth.

Though she would have liked to stay and pester Felix about the mysterious magic he was working, she knew when she was being dismissed. She disliked it a great deal, as the old resentment born of abysmal treatment from her village still tickled the back of her mind. Nevertheless, she pushed it aside. Felix was working towards freeing them from the Companion. Slowing him down with questions was not in her best interest. Nor was he intentionally ignoring her, she knew that. What she wasn't so sure of was if she wanted his attention, as the Companion twisted and skewed their emotions.

"Are you feeling all right?" Artyem asked, sensing

her inner struggle as they wended their way through the library and back into the magnificent corridors of the castle. Perhaps she was acting more like Felix now too.

"I don't know what I'm feeling anymore," she admitted. "I don't know what emotions are mine and which are Felix's. It's making me anxious. Or is Felix anxious?"

"You're both anxious," he said sagely. "Rightfully so, too. There is no guarantee there is a way to release you from this bond."

Emya's heart fluttered fearfully at this revelation. It was a possibility she didn't care to consider. She was about to say as much when a trio of ornately dressed women approached them, stopped, and curtsied to Emya. Struck by surprise, Emya gawked and then sent a pleading look to Artyem.

"What do I do?" she asked.

He shrugged. The ladies seemed to expect her to do something, so she dipped an awkward and shaky courtesy. Their faces lit up with delight and they smiled and tittered in their own language as they moved on.

"I told you," said a familiar, amused voice. "You needn't do anything."

Prince Othilrin sauntered up and bowed to Emya, his expression of amusement deepening as he saw her discomfort increase. Her cheeks flushed with even more embarrassment knowing that Felix could feel she was with the prince again.

"No need to bow to me then," she said with annoyance.

"I apologize," he said, intoning sincerity. "I am used to dealing with Felix's brand of dry humor and I have to admit it has ruined me."

"Well that's alright then," Emya said with a hint of sarcasm but she was smiling despite herself.

"I'm glad to hear. Seeing as you have abandoned Felix, no doubt for your own sanity, would you care to join me for a little tour of the castle?"

"Sure," she said, as she did not dare refuse him regardless of whatever he said about her rank. When he took her arm in his, she caught a glimpse of Artyem frowning deeply.

She had little time to consider what he was upset by and quickly dismissed it as Artyem's typical skepticism. The prince whisked her through the castle, stopping to show her ballrooms, dining rooms, courtrooms, and more. Emya was overwhelmed by the grandeur.

"And that concludes our tour of the inner palace. I think that's enough for today, seeing as a tour of the whole castle would take half the night and it's late already."

Indeed, she found as they passed a large, glass window, night had fallen. The sky was now bright with stars reflecting off a vast, shimmering lake.

"It's magnificent," she breathed.

"A fine compliment. I think I tend to take it for granted since I live here. I know I shouldn't and seeing the palace through your eyes is a refreshment I sorely needed."

She had been referring to the lake but decided not to tell him, as her opinion of the palace could not be put into words.

"There is one more thing I want to show you," he said.

Artyem, who'd been a silent, deferring presence throughout the tour spoke up now. "I think it can wait. I'm sure Emya is hungry for dinner."

"Ah, perhaps you're right," said the prince.

"What is it though?" Emya said, perceiving it was something Artyem didn't want her to see.

The prince looked at Artyem's grim expression and sighed. "Something I probably shouldn't show you."

"Then I want to see it," she said, ignoring the sharp look from Artyem. If he was against it, then it likely had something to do with magic.

The Prince smiled. "Your wish is my command."

Chapter Two

Up they climbed, step after step, around a wide square tower at the center of the palace. The stairs were encased in a narrow corridor that wound around the outer walls. Windows looked out over the palace, and as they climbed higher, Emya was astounded by the sprawling structure of gold stone walls sparkling in the light of high lamps and the rosy spires glowing in the moon light. Even Artyem couldn't hide his astonishment behind his carefully neutral expression.

It did not come as a surprise that she was the only one out of breath as they neared the top, though Artyem looked a little bit smug as she gasped for air. Finally, they arrived at a small landing with beautifully ornate doors, behind which was the prince's private study, so he said. He did not take them inside it, instead leading them through a small, unassuming door in the corner. As unassuming as a door could be in the magnificent palace. Behind it was a small, short staircase Emya was dismayed to find, and at the top, in contrast to everything else in the palace, was a heavy, iron door in a sturdy frame. The prince knocked lightly, and after a few moments, it slowly swung open. Bright light filled the corridor beyond, as though the sun shined beyond despite the darkness of night.

Inside, as best as she could understand it, was a forest. Stout, thick trunks sprouted from a pool of crystal-clear water that swirled and eddied around them. The trees floated in the water. Their crowns were a light green color, almost aqua. Their leaves bobbed gently, and their roots swayed listlessly in the pool. Their trunks were light brown and glowing with a white light that shone through the crevices in their bark, visible despite the bright light shining overhead. Casting her gaze up, it seemed to Emya that the source of the light was the ceiling itself.

"I've never seen anything like this," she said. The prince smiled appreciatively.

"Few have. There are no more trees like them in the world."

"There never really were," Artyem said. "But the closest species died out a thousand years ago."

"Yes. Floating trees were brought here over a

25

thousand years ago. They are also known as the Source of Magic Trees, and they're so rich in magical energy that you can see it glowing in their bark."

Emya had learned that some rare plants contained magic. Some mages searched the world for such plants, carefully dug them up, and replanted them in secret locations. The Citadel had one such plant, a flower, though when she'd seen it, it hadn't shown any signs of being particularly magical.

"The ancient sorcerers nearly destroyed them all in their quest for power. My ancestors brought one here and nurtured it until the rivers and lakes of this country were full of them," said the prince. "That's why Asulashio was one of the only kingdoms never to be conquered by the sorcerers."

He bowed his head and sighed, swiping away a lock of hair that fell over his face.

"Then your ancestors tried to use the magic from the trees to conquer. That's why the Citadel forbids mages from helping you," Emya said softly.

"Yes, and while it was a considerable blow to be denied help from the Citadel, the loss of so many of these trees, thousands of them decimated in less than a decade, has been my country's true punishment."

Artyem nodded solemnly.

"I accept the Citadel's decision from all those years ago. I understand why they did it, but I can't let these trees die out. I need the mages of the Citadel to help get these trees out of this vault and return them to the kingdom where all my people can enjoy them. And, if the stories are true, the trees will be able to enjoy my people as well."

"What's that supposed to mean?" Artyem asked.

"Oh, it's an old wive's tale that claimed that the trees were aware of people and could tell when one was good and kind or bad and deceitful. As my people approached with the intent of harvesting them for their magic it was said that the trees became restless and appeared to swim away, causing gentle rivers to become swift rapids."

"So then why don't you give the trees to the Citadel?" Emya asked. "Since they already know how to take care of them."

"Ah," he said with a sly grin towards Artyem. "Now that is why, I'm sure, Artyem didn't want me to show you this. These trees aren't in this vault simply for their own protection. They play an important role here. Their magic leaches into the water, you see. We have a system of pumps and drains which circulate the water from the river below up into this tower and then back. This provides enough magic to keep our crops from failing, heals our sick, and is used in many rituals. A small cup is enough to quench your thirst for a whole day in a drought."

"And not in a drought?" Artyem interrupted. The prince laughed and shrugged.

"The same, but it is too precious now to have everyone in the kingdom drinking it every day. This water and these trees are essential to my people's lives. We cannot give these trees away. Moreover, if we can make these trees as they once were, their magic will endure beyond the kingdom and will bring prosperity back to other lands. It will help heal the world of the damage done by those who abused magic."

"I see," Emya said. "That doesn't sound too bad."

"No," he agreed. "It doesn't"

~~*~*~*~*

They walked back down the stairs and the prince excused himself, claiming fatigue. Emya walked with Artyem back to the library.

"There is no point acclimating ourselves to the time change until we know how long we'll be here," Artyem said, his soft voice amplified in the deserted corridors.

"Strange, I feel as though you should be insisting I get some rest."

Artyem smiled. "That is how you think of me, is it not?"

"I have a question."

"I shall answer to the best of my knowledge."

"Why didn't you want me to see those trees? They're amazing. Is it because they're magic?"

"No," he said flatly. "It's as Prince Othilrin said. I did

28

not want him to tell you about his plans for the trees, magic, the kingdom. His intention, though honorable, was to win you to his side. You're a mage of the Citadel and a friend of Felix, therefore you must have some influence over the decision the mage will make regarding his request. Though you are entitled to form your own opinion, I did not feel it was appropriate for him to try and influence."

Emya, confused and a little shocked, shook her head. "But I don't have any influence over anything. I've only been a mage of the Citadel a short while."

"Which is why I did not forbid it outright. It won't hurt for you to see the trees and hear his tale; however, I did not want to burden you with more troubles. As to your influence, while you may not be a Mistress of the Citadel, your friendship with Felix gives you considerably more clout than you realize. He may not turn to you for exceptional wisdom and knowledge, but he would rather listen to someone he likes and trusts than anyone else. Though that is not always possible."

"Does he not like and trust the Masters?"

Artyem started to reply and stopped himself. "Listen to me, claiming to preserve you from unnecessary troubles and I go and start one all on my own. He does trust the Masters. He turns to them for knowledge and wisdom, so there must be some trust in that regard. In other regards, it's more complicated, especially compared to how much simpler it would be for him to listen to you and me."

Emya was quiet the rest of the walk to the library, mulling over the many complicated things she'd heard that day, trying to puzzle them out into some sort of cohesive whole. The Masters did not want to grant the kingdom mages, so Felix would find no support there. It would certainly be simpler if he had only to ask Emya if the request should be granted, but she knew nothing about it. Placing the decision on someone who knew so little was foolish and reckless. The matter required the kind of knowledge and wisdom of many master mages and Felix was smart enough to see that. So why did he not trust them?

As they entered the library's vault, they found Felix sitting cross-legged on the floor, a book in his hands.

"Back already?" Felix said without looking up.

"Couldn't keep the prince out all night," Emya replied.

That got Felix's attention. He looked up at her and grinned. "That's surprising. I've known him to stay up many a night until dawn."

"Maybe he stayed up last night?" she offered.

"Perhaps."

"Have you given up on the scroll?" Artyem said with a gesture to the book.

"This? No, I've been trying to find a translation to an obscure word I've forgotten, or never really knew. How was your tour?"

Emya was about to answer but Artyem cut in. "He showed her the trees."

Felix raised his brow. "You let him?"

"I objected, but that only increased her curiosity."

"Did it?" he laughed and turned to Emya. "What did you think?"

"I thought they were wonderful," she said. "It's a pity they keep them locked away."

"I agree. Do you think Civim should help the kingdom grow more?"

Emya shrugged, dropping onto the floor across from him. "Why not? If what he said is true, it would help other lands, not just this kingdom."

"That is true," Felix said and frowned. "The problem is, what's to stop anyone from harvesting the trees and using their magic? We could be right back where we started in a few hundred years, maybe fewer if others can find a way to make them grow faster. That's the problem. The Masters are so afraid of what might happen, that they'd almost rather let the trees die off. I can't convince them otherwise unless Othilrin can come up with a way to ensure they won't be misused, which seems unlikely. I am far more reluctant to let the trees die off, however. So far, they are the only known natural magical sources that also reabsorb raw magic. They might be the key to solving that problem. Though the Masters believe a stricter control of magic would suffice in that respect."

"It would still be a shame if they were gone," Emya said resolutely.

"Agreed."

"How much longer is this going to take?" She gestured to the scrolls.

"Not too long I hope, once I find this word. Are you hungry? Artyem could take you to get something to eat."

"I'm tired of walking," she said, stretching out her feet so they tapped Felix's knees, causing a small smile to cross his lips. "My feet hurt. That was almost as hard as the trek to the Citadel."

"Why don't you rest here and distract Felix for a while?" Artyem said, "I'll see about having some food brought over here."

With neither objecting, Artyem disappeared. Emya sat and watched Felix read for a little while. Then she got up and looked at the scrolls. Finding them completely incomprehensible, she sat next to Felix and attempted to read over his shoulder. The book, of course, was also not in a language she understood.

"Sorry I haven't been much company lately." He looked up from the book into space. "I've never been much company to you, have I?"

"What do you mean?" she asked, flicking absently at a small, loose piece of stone.

"I've been either mostly incapacitated or busy with other things. I don't think I saw you at all except to talk about the Companion while we were at the Citadel."

"We spent a lot of time together on the trip up the mountain."

"Yeah." He set the book aside and leaned back on his hands, peering at the ceiling. "I think that's when I started to think of you as a friend."

"That's nice, but I've never thought of you as a friend."

He smirked bitterly. "I don't blame you."

"This whole time I've been waiting for you to betray me and steal my magic using the object."

"That's not unfair."

"I'm kidding."

He opened his mouth in a surprised 'oh' and then laughed. "Good, though that's not a very funny joke considering you did try to run away from me and the Citadel."

"Yes, but only because I thought you had betrayed me, and I didn't trust the Masters. I'm still not sure I do. I have worried about it a little, but for the most part, I think I've considered you a friend when you helped me escape."

"Good, I'm glad," he said with a disarming grin.

He picked up the book and flipped absently through the pages as though he had something else to say but didn't know how. She could feel his tension. Emya leaned against the wall. They sat in silence until Artyem returned, as Felix returned his focus to the book after a few minutes. Emya could feel the moment when he pushed aside whatever weighed so heavily on his heart.

"This was all I could get," Artyem said with a smirk, his arms loaded with a blanket-covered basket. He set it on the floor, spread out the blanket, and unloaded the basket. Out came three loaves of grain-coated brown bread, a slab of butter, an overflowing dish of sharp-smelling cheese, freshly carved meats, grapes, apples, and berries, both fresh and in the form of tarts. From the bottom of the basket, he pulled a canteen of water, a bottle of wine, and three golden goblets.

"Artyem, you utter failure," Felix said, shaking his head in all seriousness. "How are we supposed to sustain ourselves on these meager rations?"

"This is all the kitchen could give me. They extend their sincerest apologies."

Felix tore a chunk of bread off and buttered it generously. "We'll make the best of it."

"I take it there is some joke I'm missing?" Emya asked biting into a berry tart. Its light crust and delicate flavor rivaled anything from Civim.

"If we have time to attend the banquet they have every night, you'll see," Felix said. "These courtiers spare no expense or luxury."

When they'd eaten their fill, there were still several meals worth of food leftover. Emya lounged against the wall, her belly uncomfortably full.

"I've never been starved," she mused. "Except as punishment, but I always knew I wouldn't be starved to

34

death. Yet I never imagined such food existed, or that I'd eat so much of it."

"Your life has changed drastically over the past few months," Artyem said. "Are you alright?"

"I take it one day at a time," she replied.

"One crisis at a time," Felix added.

"I've lived my whole life one crisis at a time," Artyem said. "I can't say it gets easier though."

"My life was never easy, I don't see why that should change," Emya said in agreement, but the looks on Felix and Artyem's faces told her it was a joke. Embarrassed, she looked at her feet.

"Oh!" Felix said suddenly, getting to his feet. "Of course, the word is passage. How could I have forgotten?"

"Passage?" Emya asked.

"Yes." Felix bent over the scrolls. "As in, the passage of time."

After several moments he looked up, a smug smile playing across his features. "I can do the spell now. Thanks, Emya, talking to you always helps."

"Any time." Emya got up as Felix turned to stand before the wall she was lounging against. From his pocket, he produced a dagger. Emya thought he was going to cut himself, or someone else, but instead he drew it against the wall, though lightly enough that it didn't leave a mark, and mumbled in the ancient language. Light glowed from the dagger's path, as it dipped and rose, whirled, and danced in Felix's nimble fingers. When he finished off a point near the floor and stood back, the light shined brightly for a moment then faded. The stone wall was unchanged except for a small rectangular piece of stone gone missing. Felix gripped the stone through the hole and pulled. A door-shaped portion of the wall swung open.

Beyond the door was nothing to be excited about, and given their reason for being there, Emya felt more apprehensive than interested in a vault of dangerous magic books. The small room was lined entirely in bluestone, shimmering in the torchlight Felix produced with a flick of his hand. In shelves carved in the stone walls held a modest collection of bound books and parchment scrolls, with most of the shelves left bare. Emya supposed they'd built the room intending to add more books. Dangerous books which hadn't been found, or more unsettling, hadn't been written yet.

"This is the largest collection?" she asked.

"These books contain the most secret and sometimes dangerous information in their collection. These books are forbidden to be copied or moved from this vault."

When the door snapped shut behind them, Emya looked around and found Artyem had not come in.

"Where's Artyem?" she asked.

"He's not allowed in here."

"Because he's not a mage?"

"Because no one except the Masters of Civim is

allowed in here."

"Should I leave then?"

He shook his head, strolling around the shelves. "I won't tell if you won't. Besides, I need your help."

He stopped at the shelf at the end of the vault, then he reached up and pulled a heavy tome off the top shelf. Emya hurried over to help him. He handed it to her and motioned her to stand back. A moment later a sturdy table surrounded by plush armchairs appeared.

"Can't do magic in the outer vault, except the spell to open it," he said. "Otherwise the door won't appear. But once you're in here it doesn't matter anymore, does it?"

Emya set the heavy book on the table and fell into a chair.

"Oh," she said in surprise as she opened the book. "This is in my language."

"Yes. That whole shelf is. So, you work on those, and I'll read through the rest."

Emya turned her attention to the book resolutely, but by the third page, she realized what a boring task it was going to be. The language was archaic and high-minded, and while her already poor reading skills had improved since she began studying at Civim, she still struggled with the texts designed for intermediate students.

"Felix," she said after an hour or so, "I'm sorry but I don't understand this."

37

He looked up with a hint of amusement.

"I didn't think you would. I don't entirely understand most of it."

"Then how am I supposed to be helping?"

"Look for anything that sounds like the Companion or magic that connects two mages," he said flipping the page of his book with an impatient flick.

"I'll try." She turned dutifully back to the book.

~~*~*~*~*

It took a long time to get through half the books. Three days in total, but it felt much longer. Though they found little in the way of helpful material. At least no evil creatures, attracted to the Companion attacked the palace while they worked.

"It's because we spend so much time in this vault. It shields the contents from any magical connection, inside or out," Felix explained. "Essentially nothing outside the vault can sense the Companion in here."

"Is this where we'll keep it once we're free?"

"No, there is a much more powerfully protected vault in Civim where I plan to put it."

He shifted uncomfortably in his seat. If it was anyone else, she would have assumed it was because of sitting in the same place too long. But because of her connection through the Companion, she knew there was something he was afraid to tell her.

"Oh, just spit it out," she said sharply. Felix glared at her and she felt both their tempers flare. She'd grown used to their connection and was learning how to control her emotions well enough to keep things civil. "Please tell me what's bothering you."

"I didn't want to alarm you, but that's the other reason I need you in here with me. I'm not sure what would happen if one of us is in the vault and the other is outside. Whoever doesn't have the Companion might pass out, but knowing the nature of the vault, it might be much worse."

"Do you think the vault could break the connection entirely?" she asked, excitement dashed by his reply.

"Yes, it could, but that would almost certainly kill one of us."

That explained a lot. Over the past three days, any time Emya said she needed to leave the vault Felix also left with her.

Deciding not to argue about it, she turned back to her book. It was a dusty old tome written by a mage whose main interest had been the floating trees, which kept her attention pretty well even though it didn't seem to be a source of useful information. As she flipped the page, however, a name caught her eye. She read on eagerly then turned to Felix.

"I think I found something," Emya said.

"What?" He looked up, his features glazed. It wasn't the first time she had said this.

"My name."

"Your name?"

"My family name, Messam…Pike Messam."

"The sorcerer?"

"Yes, the author mentions that he consulted Pike Messam for advice on extracting magic from the floating trees. He says Messam's work mainly focused on putting magic back into objects, though he knew very well how to extract it."

Felix pulled the book from her and peered at the passage.

"This must be at least a century before the Great War," he said. "No one would be able to 'consult' with Pike Messam once he came to real power."

"Look at the last passage." She pointed to the bottom of the page. "He says Messam can make an object that can extract the magic from the trees and the author could direct it into himself, but the object would connect to his natural power, and he worries that would leave him open for someone, like Messam, to take the power."

"Sounds familiar," Felix said excitedly.

"So how do we look further into this? Did Messam write any of these books?"

"No. None of these books were written by the sorcerers. Those books are locked away in the strongholds in the Twisted Realm." Felix furrowed his brow and pursed his lips.

"The Twisted Realm?" Emya asked in confusion.

"Yes, you've heard of it. The place where the great magic battles were fought that scarred the whole world. It's a desolate place saturated in raw magic. All the sorcerers' strongholds are contained within. I was afraid we might have to go there."

"But wouldn't a book written by the sorcerer who made the companion tell of a way to break its bond?"

"Most likely, but we need to figure out which sorcerer created the Companion if we can. It's too difficult and dangerous to go wandering into the Twisted Realm without knowing which stronghold we're trying to find. They are all magically hidden and protected. There are plenty of histories on the sorcerers in the library though. Let's see if there's anything useful on Pike Messam."

They returned their piles of scrolls and books to the shelves and hurried out of the vault and into the great library. Emya gazed up as she followed Felix through the maze of spiraling bookcases, like great tree trunks, buttresses branched out, creating a bare winter canopy.

"How are you going to find the books we need in all this?" she asked.

"There are caretakers who know the library inside and out. They can tell you the location of any book whether you know the title or not." He turned a smug smile at her over her shoulder. "We don't need them though, because I know this place as well as they do."

Finding the spiral he was looking for, he led her up

the winding staircase. As she climbed, Emya held onto a banister with ivy carved into the rich dark wood. Up and up they climbed. Emya held her chin high, keeping her eyes away from the ground. Felix chuckled at what must have made her look very high and mighty. Well, she was high, that was for sure.

"Afraid of heights, are you?"

"I'm afraid of many things, why shouldn't a great distance to fall be one of them?"

His smile widened. "I know you're afraid often because I can feel it. It might interest you that several of the masters and mistresses have observed that you are quite resilient. More so than others who have come from a situation not nearly as bad as yours. If you or I told them how you truly feel, they would be very surprised."

"You haven't told them?"

"Nope." He shook his head. "It's not my place."

He pulled on an old tome with dark, blood-red leather binding. Though the cover was worn, and the pages yellowed, there was not a speck of dust. He held it out for her to take. The smell of old parchment filled her nose as she opened it. The writing was indecipherable, as she had expected. She closed it and accepted another smaller book. Felix selected three more books that he carried and motioned her to lead the way down.

It was much harder to keep her eyes up on the way down, but she summoned the resilience her teachers had seen. Though now she was afraid and embarrassed that Felix knew how scared she was.

When they reached the last few steps, she sped down them with a sigh of relief. She turned to gaze up at where they'd been and wondered how Felix managed to climb up all those stairs often enough to know where all the books were.

"Hey," she said sharply as realization struck her. He looked at her with a brow arched. "You're afraid of heights too!"

"I was wondering when you were going to figure that out," he said with a cheeky grin.

Setting the books on the nearest table, Emya sat and waited for Felix to peruse them, for none were in her language. He flipped through the pages, almost heedless of their delicacy in age. He must have read the books before.

"Here we go," he said after some time. "This book references a historian who wrote in the times shortly after the war."

He stood up and turned on the spot. "That would be... Over here."

Emya followed him up another spiral, though they only went up halfway, to retrieve another book. So it went for the rest of the night and most of the morning. Though light shone in, and the library came to life with visitors, Emya's lids drooped, and her head nodded.

"Ah, this is it!" Felix said suddenly. Several people sitting nearby looked over at them with irritation.

"Sorry," Felix whispered and continued in a low voice. "This historian was allowed an audience with Messam near the end of the war, shortly before Messam disappeared."

Emya, now fully awake, nodded eagerly for him to go on. "I thought that was impossible."

"So did I, but apparently Messam had something he needed to tell the outside world. There aren't too many details about his work. If there were, this would have been in the vault. It seems Messam wasn't entirely privy to what was happening beyond the walls of his fortress. He didn't realize the lengths other sorcerers had gone to in their war for power and magic. He expressed regret for what his work contributed to and..." He tapped the page emphatically, clearly excited. "He said he was working on something to help undo some of his creations. Creations that were meant for taking magic out of the natural world but were used to take magic from mages."

"Does it say if he finished it?"

"No, the historian never heard from him, or anyone associated with him after that."

"But he might have."

"He might. It's not much to go on, but I think it's our best shot."

"No, it's not much to go on." Artyem stood behind them. He'd arrived so stealthily that Emya hadn't noticed him until that moment. "Please don't tell me you're planning a trip out into the Twisted Realm on the musings of a half-mad sorcerer."

Felix huffed a sigh. "They were all mad. Completely insane. But yes, I am."

"I suppose that makes sense, seeing as you're completely insane too."

"You knew this was the plan from the start, Artyem."

"And I've been against it from the start. I had hoped you'd do better to convince me it was a good idea though."

"Sorry to disappoint." Felix stood up and stacked the books on the table. With a flick of his hand, the books flew away into the library back to their shelves. A dozen faces turned to stare at them. Several richly adorned men scurried around spirals to see who had performed the magic. "We could stay here for years reading every book in this library and not find anything more promising."

"Is that why you're abandoning all subtlety?" Artyem asked.

"No." Felix looked around at all the gawking faces. "Habit."

Artyem sighed, eyes closed, and rubbed the bridge of his nose with one finger. "I know it's pointless to argue."

"That's correct."

"So, answer me this, are we bringing Emya?"

"We must. You know that."

"And exactly how do you plan to keep her alive in that forsaken land?"

Felix grumbled. "I'm getting tired of being asked that question."

"Well, now you must have an answer because I will not allow you to take her to the most dangerous place in the world completely unprepared."

"You can't stop me," Felix said in a low, chilling voice. A shiver ran down Emya's spine.

"I know. But you must live with the consequences if you do. If you survive."

Felix bowed his head and crossed his arms.

"I know," he said. Then, looking frustrated but determined, he added, "I'll have a plan by tomorrow morning."

Chapter Three

Artyem led Emya and Felix to their suite of rooms. Emya dropped onto a couch of fine, cream-colored fabric stuffed with feathers and sweet-smelling herbs. A pot of fragrant tea steamed on the low table beside her. Felix poured some into a delicate ceramic cup and handed it to her before pouring his own and sitting on the couch across from her. Artyem disappeared to see to whatever business a guard of the citadel had in a kingdom on the other side of the world. Or perhaps he was angry at Felix for speaking to him as though he was the enemy.

Emya scowled into her tea. Artyem was overly fixated on protecting her from whatever perils lay ahead, considering the Companion put her and Felix in danger every moment of every day. If he was really Felix's friend, why wouldn't he be more supportive? Emya gazed around the sitting room in silence while she sipped her tea, each warm mouthful calmed her spirit and cleared her addled thoughts.

"He thinks we're all going to die in the Twisted Realm," Emya said at last. "Artyem."

Felix smiled wryly. "Can you blame him?"

"I would think a better friend would do everything he can to help us."

"I think a better friend would try harder to stop us."

Emya set her cup down, the impulse to throw her arms up rising rapidly with her temper.

"Are you joking?" she said hotly. "We must break the connection."

"Yes, and the sooner the better, as we both know, but no one else can entirely understand that. They believe we could hide the object, and stay in the safety of Civim until we can find a safer way to remove it." Felix slumped in his chair, throwing his head back to gaze at the ceiling. "If I wasn't connected to it, I think I would believe that too. It's not the first time we've dealt with a dangerous magic object, but I know, this one is different. It can't be protected."

Emya couldn't argue with that. The anger drained out of her as quickly as it had come upon her. Felix visibly relaxed too. He was much better at not letting her emotions take hold of him.

"So…" A deep yawn overcame her. "So, what are we going to do?"

Felix's eyelids drooped, and he fell slowly onto the couch. "I don't know."

His eyes closed and his breathing slowed. Emya stretched out along the couch and soon followed Felix into sleep.

~~*~*~*~*

Felix didn't have a plan the next day, as it turned out, and he didn't believe he needed one, which he grumbled about whenever the topic came up. However, Artyem suggested, and Felix agreed, that they should pass the time training Emya in defensive magic and that they should attempt to map out the fastest possible path.

"Not the safest?" Emya asked as they discussed it over a decadent breakfast.

"There is nowhere safe in that place," Felix said.

"What's it like exactly?" she asked.

"I've only ever gone just past the border," Felix said. "It's like a desert from what I've seen. From the few accounts recorded, and none of them recent, those who dwell there are mad. The saturation of raw magic drove them to a state like your village."

Emya gaped at him in shock and surprise.

"There are people living there? I thought it would

49

be unlivable like the red forest."

"No one from the outside can live there, like the red forest, but these people never left and somehow survived. Of course, there are the creatures that roam the land, sustained on the raw magic as well."

Emya couldn't begin to imagine what those people might be like, but she was certain she didn't want to find out.

While Artyem spent his days in the library pouring over old maps and records of the Twisted Realm, plotting their way, Emya began the arduous task of learning to fight with magic.

It required the combination of strength magic with elemental magic. The only kind of elemental magic she had experience with was fire and even so she could do very little with it. She had to use her strength and magic to enhance the elemental energy. No matter how many times Felix explained it, Emya could not grasp the elements well enough to mold and direct them. It was like trying to catch rain in a colander.

At the end of a week of lessons, Felix had managed to teach her to make a shield out of air. If she couldn't help him fight, at least he didn't have to worry about protecting her, so he'd said when she almost fried him with a ball of white-hot magic she'd produced on accident.

Despite that incident, he still wanted to teach her how to summon fire, since she already had a knack for it. Many magical creatures could be harmed by fire. Its destructive force often overcame them before they could stop it or harness it.

The prince watched them practice sometimes, with Felix's permission. As Emya, frustrated and tired, failed to produce a complex burst of power and air, meant to knock her opponent away, the prince applauded at the gentle breeze that ruffled Felix's hair.

"That's not what I was supposed to do," Emya growled at him. The prince laughed.

"I know, I'm just being supportive. Wish I could do that."

Emya found it disconcerting to have believed she had nothing of value her entire life and yet the possession she had resented having most was coveted by a powerful prince. It wasn't that long ago she would have traded her magic to him for anything if she could. In a sense, she had traded it to the Kings for a little acceptance.

And the Kings had tried to take her magic from her. If the prince knew about the companion, he could have his wish. At this thought, she looked nervously away from the prince's admiring gaze. He must have thought she was being shy or modest because he tactfully excused himself and strode off to do princely things.

"This is pointless," she said to Felix in frustration. She sat down on the warm stone of the courtyard. "It's going to take too long for me to learn enough to be of any help. I can barely protect myself."

Felix smiled wryly sitting next to her. "I know. But it will make Artyem happy. Besides, when we return to the citadel, you will have advanced much further in elemental magic than you would have if you'd stayed. I am an excellent teacher."

Emya smirked. His endless patience was his best skill, though he did explain complex things clearly.

"If that's so, then maybe I should become your apprentice."

"I wouldn't mind that. I don't think the masters will allow it though."

Attuned as she was to his emotions now, she appreciated his genuine excitement at the idea of teaching her every day.

"I don't understand why you have to listen to them," she said. "If you're going to be their leader someday, won't they have to listen to you? Can't you just tell them you're going to teach me?"

"Well, I'm not their leader yet. Even when I am, I won't be able to do everything I want. If I don't listen to them, they can remove me from leadership."

"But surely teaching me would not take up too much time?"

Felix's amused expression turned to surprise.

"By the time I become the leader you won't need a formal teacher. You might be a mistress yourself."

"Oh. It sounded as though you would be the leader

very soon."

"Ten to twenty years is soon, for mages. We do tend to live longer than people without magic. Master Kyn is almost three hundred years old."

"Really?" Emya had no idea magic made one live longer. Then again, she had been lied to her entire life, believing that magic would destroy her and everyone around her. "Does that mean you stay young longer or look older longer?"

Felix laughed. "It depends on the mage, but in general I'd say we age more slowly."

"Well, I guess I have that to look forward to if we survive the Twisted Realm."

"We will," Felix reassured her. "Have courage. We will survive as long as we can outrun Artyem."

Emya laughed. Felix jumped up and held out his hand to her.

"Come. Let's find our skeptic friend. It's time for dinner."

They made their way toward the library. That evening they were to dine with the prince. Felix promised it would be a spectacular dinner. Emya believed him, and it only made her more nervous. Any time she spent with the prince made her feel like a fraud. As though he would find out about her humble beginnings and become angry that he treated such an unimportant person with such deference. Felix reassured her, any time she brought it up, that she was important in the prince's eyes, but she found that much harder to believe.

They found Artyem bent over three maps spread out on a large table.

"Are you done throwing sparks at each other?" Artyem asked without looking up.

"Sparks and wind, yes we're done for the day," Felix said. "How are the maps coming?"

"It would be more productive if we had any current maps," Artyem said carefully rolling up yellowed parchment before him. "These are centuries-old copies of thousand-year-old maps."

"Are you volunteering for an expedition to redraw the maps?" Felix asked.

"No," Artyem said shortly. "I am only pointing out that my preparations may be for naught."

"This whole endeavor may be for naught but we must try."

"Must we?"

"Are you going to have this argument again?" Emya cut in irritably.

Felix shot her a surprised look.

"No," he said. "There's nothing to argue about."

Artyem's features hardened but changed the subject.

"The prince would like to be informed of our plans."

"I don't think we have any obligation—"

"Any disruption we may cause will likely fall on his kingdom," Artyem said. "We owe him that courtesy."

"Fine. We can discuss it over dinner."

"Very well."

Artyem swept from the room. Emya watched his retreat. The tension between him and Felix increasingly worried her. From beside her came a tired sigh.

"You agree with Artyem don't you?" Felix asked. "You think this is a hopeless endeavor?"

"No," Emya said slowly. "That is, I don't know. All I know is that I don't want to be connected to the Companion any longer. I'm worried that this feud between you is going to distract you from the dangers."

Felix gave her a small smile from over the maps his finger traced along.

"Ah. I forget that you don't know us as well as we know each other. Don't worry. Artyem may disagree but he is one of the best men I could hope to have fighting beside me."

Felix straightened up and strode off after Artyem. Emya followed. They found Artyem leaning against the wall down the hall, looking out the window. He fell in step beside Felix

"What sort of trouble does the prince expect us to cause?" Emya asked, continuing their conversation.

Felix shrugged. "I honestly couldn't say. No one knows what goes on in there, but for some reason, it doesn't spill out into the world too often. Some sort of magic is keeping it at bay, we don't know what kind."

"And we don't know which is more worrying,"

Artyem added grimly. "What is in there, or how powerful and other the magic is that holds it."

Felix nodded, grimacing.

~~*~*~*~*

They met the prince in a formal dining room. Emya had thought she had grown used to the splendors of the palace. Yet again she found herself in awe. The magnificent chamber had twelve stretching windows, the waning afternoon light shining through them glittered off the sandy gold stone floor. They sat at a long, dark table on matching chairs with dark velvet cushions. Smiling, gracious servants brought in the richest delicacies Emya had ever tasted although after eating just a few bites she found, with a little disappointment, it was so rich the flavor overwhelmed her.

"I'm sad to see you go," the prince was saying to Felix. "I hope to have the pleasure of your presence again soon."

"I'm sure you will," Felix replied.

"What kind of trouble are you going to cause me in the meantime?"

"Couldn't say," Felix said. "It is possible some demons may escape. I don't think we will do anything that causes any real trouble."

"Good to hear."

"Are demons different than the creatures that have attacked us before?" Emya asked.

"Yes," Felix said. "Demons are intelligent. They don't just attack like beasts, they plan, and scheme. They can speak to us as well. Sometimes in our languages. They are the most dangerous magical creatures."

"They can only exist outside the Twisted Realm for short periods," said the prince. "Therefore, they are rarely seen and usually only near the barrier. They are extremely dangerous if you come across one. You're only chance is to outlast it."

"There is a small guild of mages called the Infernal Keepers who deal with those creatures. It's incredible magic, and very complex," Felix said. "It's the only mage guild in the world that recruits its own members and teaches them from childhood. They visit Civim occasionally when they believe we have a good candidate, but we have no control over that guild."

"To the Master's chagrin I'm sure," the prince said with a sly grin.

"Very much," Felix said.

"We shall have to see them," Artyem said. "They like to keep track of who is entering the Twisted Realm."

Felix nodded.

"Well then. I shall escort you to the keep. It's been a while since I've visited our solitary and spooky mage friends.

"Much appreciated," said Felix.

"Spooky." Emya echoed. Othilrin chuckled.

"You'll see," he said. "Apparently living so close to the Realm gives one a certain countenance."

After dinner, the prince invited them to enjoy some music in a splendid parlor. Three musicians played soft and soothing melodies with lots of high, ringing notes. Yet it could not soothe the mixture of fear and excitement battling inside her. In the morning they would embark on the most dangerous endeavor of her life so far, though she would have Felix and Artyem who were both capable protectors. If they were successful, she would finally be free of the companion. Or dead.

As Emya followed Felix and Artyem back to their suite of rooms, dragging her feet under the weight of a most delicious meal, she could hardly imagine the dangers ahead.

~~*~*~*~*

In the early dawn light, Emya eyed the horses dubiously. She'd never ridden one. Some of her neighbors had stout, rotund, brown, and black cows they used to pull carts and plow fields. Growing up she'd seen horses a few times, and then some that Evris's neighbors owned. Now Felix expected her to ride one all the way to the border.

"Ah, there's my handsome boy."

Emya turned to find the prince, resplendent in

white and tan riding gear. He strode past her to the chestnut stallion. He gave it a treat and stroked its velvety nose while it chewed.

"Are you ready for a ride?" he asked the horse. It nickered softly in response. "Yes, it's going to be a nice ride."

Emya smiled at the exchange. While the prince communed with his horse, she looked around at the courtyard which had suddenly filled with activity. Stable hands saddled up the calmly waiting horses, while servants packed saddlebags with provisions. One of the young stable girls led a tall, broad-backed horse over to Emya.

"Are you ready my lady?" she asked. By now Emya was almost used to being addressed so formally. The look of distress that came over her was because no one seemed concerned about her complete lack of riding experience. Someone sidled up beside her, she looked up at the prince smiling kindly at her.

"I thought I'd give you a quick lesson while we wait for Felix and Artyem," he said patting the enormous animal on which she was expected to sit atop. "This is Haliss, my retired battle horse. We only fought in one short war together, thankfully, but he is the most reliable companion you could ask for. He doesn't need much guidance."

Emya was about to grumble something about how she would rather ride a smaller horse when the prince

59

swept her off her feet and placed her effortlessly into the saddle. She was so shocked at being so easily lifted that she hardly noticed the prince's unrestrained laughter.

Emya held tightly onto the saddle, expecting the animal to suddenly gallop away. Yet the horse stood completely still and gently huffed as if it could tell she had never ridden before. Emya looked around. The world felt slightly different. It wasn't being higher up. It was more a sense of suddenly being a lot taller. Though the stone paving beneath her did seem much more menacing from the back of a creature with its own will.

"Hold the reigns like this," the prince said once he had regained control of his mirth. Then he told her how to direct the horse with the press of her calf against its side. He walked next to her as the horse plodded around the courtyard. It followed her directions well enough and seemed to anticipate what she wanted it to do.

"Very good," the prince said as she came to a stop. Artyem and Felix appeared, dressed in sturdy traveling clothes.

"Hardly," Emya said sheepishly, carefully patting the horse's flank. "He did most of the work."

"That's the idea," he said, flashing his disarming smile.

"Is she ready to lead the cavalry charge?" Artyem asked softly, strapping two matching blades to the saddle of one of the waiting horses. Emya hadn't noticed his appearance.

"I don't see why not," the prince said. "She's got the best horse for it."

"I think this horse could lead the cavalry charge without me," Emya said. Artyem chuckled.

Felix came over, rolling up a map and stowing it in a leather holder. "Are we ready?"

"At your command," the prince said. "Our escort is waiting for us at the bridge."

Emya hadn't known anyone else was coming with them, though she supposed the prince couldn't wander around without guards.

"Escort? Won't that slow us down?" Felix asked.

"For a short time. Once we leave the city they shall return to their duties."

"Are you not afraid of bandits and the like?" Felix asked.

"Not with a mage in the company," he winked. Felix grinned. Emya wondered what she was missing.

While Felix and Artyem climbed onto their horses the prince exchanged a few words with his steward, then gracefully leaped and swung into his saddle. Emya's breath caught. She thought the horse would panic and gallop off, but it didn't so much as twitch. The prince caught her eye and winked.

"I thought that would impress you," the prince said. "I guess it just scared you."

"I am impressed," Emya said, "Impressed that you didn't break your neck."

61

They both laughed.

"You could shoot an arrow through an apple between these horses' ears and they wouldn't flinch," the prince said as the horses slowly clopped out of the courtyard. "We have some of the finest horse trainers in the world."

As they rode through the pathways of the castle grounds, courtiers and servants bowed and curtsied. The fragrance of flowers coated in early morning dew perfumed the air. Little songbirds chirped musically along with the gentle beat of the horses' hooves. A sweet kind of sadness filled her to leave the beautiful palace. She resolved to return one day to see the magical water trees again.

As she rode beside Felix, with Artyem and the prince ahead of them, chatting about the duties of the guards of Civim, Emya came to a realization.

"They're friends, aren't they?" she said in a low voice, leaning over slightly to Felix and pointing at their two companions.

"Yes," Felix said. "I take it you mean their friendship transcends rank."

"They almost seem like brothers," Emya said, who had never seen Artyem as relaxed and chatty with anyone other than Felix. Though she hadn't noticed it at the palace, she supposed that it was more her presence that drew up Artyem's guard. She supposed she didn't notice it before because of his scruples with the prince's opinions concerning magic. Yet, having scruples with magic didn't stop Artyem from being friends with anyone.

"In a way, they are like brothers. Othilrin came to Civim to train with the Tritium Guards for two years. He was one of the few outsiders allowed the privilege. Although I suppose everyone is an outsider before they become a guard, but he wasn't required to join the ranks after training."

"What do you mean?" Emya knew very little about the Tritium Guards. "How does one become a guard?"

"Students are brought to train and join the guard, just as mages are brought to the citadel. Often, they are orphans of war, not plague or famine as those leave children too weak. Some are the children of the guards as well. Artyem is both. His father was a guard and his mother was a young woman from this kingdom. He was born here but when his father was called back to Civim, his mother couldn't go with him. I don't know why. Artyem was raised in this city until he was seven. His mother died and he was brought to Civim."

"So Artyem knew him as the prince of his home country?" Emya asked.

"More than that. They knew each other personally. His mother was a healer who was often summoned to the palace to care for the queen. Both she and the queen died a week apart."

Emya didn't need Felix to describe two young boys

devastated by the loss of their mothers. She could easily picture it from her own experience not long ago.

"Artyem's father remarried. His stepmother loves him very much and treats him as her own son. She was his main support when—" Felix seemed to catch himself. "Well, let's just say she was the happiest of anyone when he joined the guard."

~~*~*~*~*

As they approached the south bridge, light glinted off the polished armor of the twelve guards awaiting them.

"Your highness," said one who appeared to be the leader. "I have sent scouts ahead, that will meet us at the border. We are ready to ride out."

The guard fell in around them as they crossed the bridge into the city proper. Once again Emya was shocked and impressed. The bustling city teemed with people. There were shops and stalls with vendors selling food, flowers, cloth, and livestock. Children ran and played, chased by happily barking dogs. Everyone moved out of their path as they went by. Most bowed, but some, Emya noticed, ignored them, or glared at them. Well not everyone liked the prince, she supposed, but maybe they knew Felix was a mage and didn't like him, or Civim for not letting the city have mages. She couldn't guess, but at least they didn't seem to want to fight the guards.

Prince Othilrin pointed out important and historic landmarks along the way. There was a large ornate statue of one of their most beloved kings. Emya didn't catch his name but he had led them through a dark time of war and famine. In a beautiful green park, citizens spent time picnicking and relaxing. And of course, there were the canals where the floating trees used to grow. The water was brown and grimy, but the prince said it had been crystal clear when the trees had been in it.

After a few hours, they left the city behind. The organized cluster of the buildings cleared away gradually to farmland and then a vast forest rose up before them. Their guard left them at the edge of the forest, promising to meet the prince at the city border upon his return. The prince waved genially to them as the four of them continued into the forest.

"Is this safe?" Emya asked looking around at the thick foliage. It was considerably darker. "Shouldn't you have a guard the whole way?"

"Few wander out here because they're afraid of the demons. Though demon occurrences are rare, they can be devastating. I would rather not risk my men. That may be too many people for Felix to protect."

"So that's what you meant by bandits?" Emya asked, remembering the confusing conversation.

"Yes," the prince said. "Magical, evil, bandits."

"The real joke is that Othilrin shouldn't be out here

at all," Artyem said. "The prince of Asulashio, wandering around a dangerous forest with nothing more than a couple of mages and one guard."

"It's certainly a scandal, but who's going to stop me?"

Artyem and Felix chuckled. Emya supposed no one was going to stop the prince except the king, but there was a certain defiant undertone in his words that suggested he still had to battle against judgments better than his own, even if they had no real power over him.

The forest was quiet. Emya's horse plodded along obediently with little direction from her. She wondered if the animal minded having someone so inexperienced at the reigns. He didn't show it, although he did shake his head when she accidentally kicked him when a spider landed on her face. Felix said very little though Artyem and the prince kept up their conversation. She glanced at him and found his expression pensive. His anxiety ate at her.

"What's the matter?" she asked in a low voice.

"Nothing," he said too quickly. Emya gave him a skeptical look.

"It's- I can't help but wonder if we're rushing into this. The Twisted Realm is dangerous beyond your imagination, and we have very little evidence that what we are looking for is in there."

Emya's brow shot up in surprise and she said indignantly, "this was your idea!"

"I know, I know," he said.

"Artyem made those very objections and you brushed them off because the danger of the companion is worth the risk. Is it not?"

"I know," he said, she didn't need to feel the pounding in her chest to know he was getting agitated.

"I'm... questioning my fitness to make this decision," he admitted with great pain. "All I want is to be free of the object. I've been tethered to it for over three years and most of that time was spent out of my mind in agony. What if I'm making a rash decision that gets us all killed?"

Emya frowned. Ahead, the prince was chatting away, but Emya couldn't tell if Artyem was listening to him or her and Felix. If he was seeking a chance to change Felix's mind, this was it. Emya wouldn't give him the chance.

"I don't think so," she said reassuringly. "It's a danger to everyone around us as well. We might get people killed if we don't attempt to find a way to remove it."

Felix smiled half-heartedly. "Maybe we're both crazy, but you're right."

Emya smiled bracingly, but a small part inside her realized when they were free of the companion, she would no longer be connected to Felix. Would they ever have these moments together after that? Would he go off with a girl like Lydia? They would always be friends, she was sure, but he was going to be the leader of Civim, and Emya had barely started learning. A heaviness filled her heart. Felix shot her a look but said nothing, for which she was grateful.

Chapter Four

The ride passed uneventfully, for which Emya was grateful. It was her first journey, she realized, that hadn't consisted of a monster attack. The sun was setting as they emerged from the foliage. Emya didn't realize they had reached the edge of the forest because an enormous wall shaded a short clearing between it and the trees.

A shadowy figure peered down at them from the ramparts. The prince waved his hand lazily and the large metal doors opened slowly and almost without sound. The echo of horse hooves on the slate was deafening in the perfect silence.

"Most of the keepers sleep during the day," Felix said in a low voice, "as the most dangerous creatures come out at night."

Emya nodded, resolving to keep her voice low. The shadowy figure from above, a man wrapped in a dark grey cloak, descended the steep steps. He lowered his hood as he approached. The horses nickered and pawed the ground nervously. Emya didn't think there was anything particularly unusual about the man, but the horses sensed something.

"Welcome your highness," the man said quietly. "And welcome to our fellow protectors of magic."

Felix, Artyem, and the prince greeted the keeper in turn. Emya had never heard any of the mages in Civim refer to themselves as protectors of magic. Was it another title for Felix? Or was it how the Keepers referred to mages? He had said *protectors,* so that must include her. She was the only other mage.

"It's been too long since you last visited, Master Felix. More than three years."

"Yes," Felix said. "I've been busy. Good to see you Dalre."

The doors whispered shut behind them. Emya suspected the only way heavy doors could be so quiet was if they were enchanted.

"We didn't expect you to journey back into the Twisted Realm so hastily after your last visit."

"I hadn't intended to," Felix said. "Unfortunately, it seems I have no other choice."

Emya glanced at Artyem just in time to see him grimace and shake his head slightly.

"Shall you leave at first light? Or is this so urgent you'll risk the dangers of the night?"

"I wish we could avoid being in there at night altogether, but our journey will take many days."

The keeper's brow shot up in surprise and he said in a warning tone, "no one has spent more than a day in that place in many decades."

"I know," Felix said. "But we must."

Artyem scowled at the ground. Only Emya noticed. The keeper's words impressed upon her the danger they were facing in a way that none of their preparations had. She was grateful that Artyem was going, despite his objections. He was truly devoted to protecting them.

Dalre, brought them inside the fortress to a small, sparsely furnished room with a beat-up old table and chairs. Another keeper brought out food, which was plain but hearty. A few more keepers, bleary-eyed and groggy, shuffled in and fell into chairs. They were perfectly polite but distant.

"Not the friendliest bunch," Felix said as they ate. "Not like our vibrant and outgoing Artyem."

Artyem rolled his eyes but did not engage.

"Maybe they don't trust outsiders," Emya said, being an authority on not trusting people herself.

"I don't know about that. I've been here dozens of times. You'd think they'd trust me by now."

"Maybe it's because every time you come here it's to enter the Twisted Realm?" Artyem said, "They don't know if you'll make it out, so they don't want to get too attached."

Felix choked on the sip of water and gave Artyem a serious look.

"You think?" he said, worry tinged his tone.

"That never crossed your mind?" Artyem said.

"I guess because I always survived."

"You've only ever gone past the barrier, and that just for a few hours. It hardly counts as going in."

"I'd never heard of magic barriers until this year," Emya mused. "And now I'm going through a second one."

"Third," Felix said. "The Kings set one up to keep the raw magic out of the council chamber."

"Oh, yes. I forgot." She didn't like being reminded of those days. Her miserable life had turned into magical chaos. The Twisted Realm was likely to be far worse than what her village had become.

"We should get some rest," Artyem said. Felix nodded.

Artyem found Dalre sitting with some other keepers. He led them to a small room with three beds.

"Where did Prince Othilrin go?" Emya asked. She hadn't noticed his absence until just then.

"Who?" Felix said, confused.

"The prince," Emya said. "I didn't see him leave."

"What prince?" Artyem asked with a slight smirk. He obviously thought Emya was teasing them.

"The-" Emya stopped, what was she talking about? Someone else was with them? No, they had journeyed to the keep alone, just the three of them.

Felix removed his cloak and boots and fell into bed with a big yawn. Emya followed suit, although she wrapped herself in her cloak, as she was suddenly very cold. It was strange, she thought as she pulled the blankets over herself. Artyem sat on his bed. He glanced around with a confused look on his face.

"It's cold," he said. "Do you need another blanket Emya?"

"No, thank you," she said, though she pulled the blankets up to her chin. "Are you alright? You look concerned."

"I have a strange feeling," Artyem said. "I'm not sure what it is."

He yawned. Emya couldn't remember if she had ever seen him yawn.

"Maybe you're just tired," she said.

"Must be," he said, but she had the feeling he was just saying that to alleviate her concern. Artyem got into bed. Emya closed her eyes and, moments later was asleep despite the shivers that had overtaken her.

~~*~*~*~*

Far too early Emya was gently shaken awake.

"Time to go, Emya," Felix said softly. "Come have

73

breakfast."

Emya sat up and rubbed her eyes. She was already dressed, and she would likely be much dirtier sooner rather than later, but it felt wrong not to change. Still, she would appreciate having an extra set of clean clothes before long, she thought as she picked up her bag and joined Felix and Artyem in the dark corridor. A different Keeper appeared and introduced himself as Ellide.

"Where is Dalre?" Emya asked softly as they followed their guide through the halls and corridors.

"He is asleep. His shift does not begin until midmorning."

Breakfast was simple, especially compared to the palace's morning delicacies. A few Keepers ate with them. Some had the tired look of those who stay up all night, and others looked as though they were just waking up.

Emya was wondering if all the Keepers wore the same uniform until she saw an old man dressed in sharp black pants and a tailcoat approach them.

"I am Vexil, Master of the Keep," he addressed Emya and Artyem. "It is good to finally meet some friends of Felix. We were beginning to think he had none."

Vexil winked conspiratorially. Emya immediately liked him.

"Why does everyone think I don't have any friends?" Felix asked with mock indignity.

"Because you're always too busy with work to make any," Artyem said.

"You always come here alone," Vexil added.

"And you only met me because you couldn't escape me," Emya piled on.

"Fair point," Felix said with a laugh.

"One of my Keepers told me you have a very long journey into the Twisted Realm ahead of you," Vexil said, his tone much more serious now.

"That's right," said Felix. "It is an urgent and dangerous matter. That is all I can tell you."

"I must warn you," Vexil lowered his voice, "there has been some strange activity within the barrier of late. I have seen some strange and dark creatures prowling close by the barrier. They do not attempt to escape, but my probes of magic have indicated they are very powerful and rife with rotten magic."

A knot of fear gripped Emya. She had heard of rotten magic but couldn't remember how it was different.

"What is rotten magic?" she whispered to Artyem.

"It's magic that has decayed, like a rotten carcass. It can have terrible effects on the world and other magic."

"I'm afraid we may be attracting them," Felix said grimly.

"My boy, if that object you carry has anything to do with them, it would be best if you left it here rather than risk the Twisted Realm."

"You sensed the Companion," Felix stated, "but you

don't know how it works."

"I do not."

"If you did, you would know we cannot leave it here," Felix said. "I believe it was found deep in the realm and I must discover where it came from and if it can be..." he paused, clearly thinking of what to tell Vexil while revealing as little as possible about how the object held his and Emya's magic in its clutches.

"If it can be destroyed without hurting people," he finished.

"And then perhaps the creatures will recede into the realm," Vexil said.

"I believe they will," Felix said. "Unless there is some great disturbance within the Twisted Realm that drives them to the barrier."

"Well then, let us hope there is not. I look forward to your success and your swift and safe return."

Felix thanked him. Vexil shook Artyem's hand and then Emya's. His grip was warm and strong but as Emya met his eyes she saw a twinge of pity. Had he discerned something about her past? Or was he just mourning the loss of a young girl to the trials of the Twisted Realm? Emya couldn't guess, but she hoped that if it was the latter, she would exceed his expectations and survive. A warm sense of purpose flared within her and she stood up from the table, as Ellide returned, ready to face whatever the Twisted Realm threw at her.

"Are you ready?" Ellide asked.

"As ready as we'll ever be," Felix said, hefting his pack.

Without another word, the stoic man led them through the dim keep to a small, sturdy metal door with a heavy padlock.

"Wait until you hear me knock. You must not go through the barrier until this door is locked once more."

Ellide took a key off a hook on the wall, unlocked the padlock, and removed it from the door. A metallic scent and a sizzling sound accompanied it. Magic, Emya realized.

With great difficulty, Ellide yanked the door open. It was much thicker and heavier than it looked, though it didn't scrape the floor.

Felix passed through first, then Artyem, and then Emya. She hadn't known what to expect. What she found before her was beyond what she ever imagined.

A wall of enormous, sinister, blood-red trees twisted and warped so thoroughly that Emya could not tell where one started and another ended. What was more unsettling was the smell. Sickly sweet, like rotting flowers and fruit. There were no leaves on the trees, but pulsing, glowing pustules oozed a dark red fluid that resembled watery sap.

"The trees are just beyond the barrier," Felix said. He led them to a small opening between two trunks, which was barely large enough for him and Artyem to squeeze through. Emya peered through into the unyielding dark.

A heavy, ringing thump made Emya jump and whirl around.

"That's our signal," Artyem said. "Are you ready, Emya?"

Exhilaration and fear sent shivers down her spine, but she steeled herself and nodded.

Felix gave her a bracing look. "It's dark and disgusting, but this is the easy part."

"That's not very comforting," Emya said. "That's like saying that however uncomfortable this is, it's only going to get worse."

"Hm, good point. Then let us say, no matter how bad things get, they will almost certainly get worse."

Artyem snorted. "Almost."

Felix led the way into the dark, Emya followed closely with Artyem behind her. She noticed that he hadn't taken his knives out, and she found this more comforting than anything either could have said.

The moment she stepped through the knotted trunks she was smothered in hot, humid, buzzing air that smelled of decay. The hair on her arms stood up. Though she took several deep breaths of the rancid air through her mouth, it felt as though very little air filled her lungs.

"This is the easy part?" Artyem gasped.

"Afraid so," Felix said. "Calm your breathing. You're getting enough air even if it doesn't feel like it."

There was no light, but the wall of trunks assured

them that they could not stray off in another direction. Something thick and gooey dripped onto Emya's arm. She wiped it off with the corner of her cloak then pulled her hood up and wrapped the cloak around herself. This proved to be futile, as the tunnel narrowed so much that they now had to turn sideways to pass through. Alongside them were trunks riddled with the puss-filled growths that burst as they slid past. Artyem coughed and gagged; Emya held her breath.

"I would much rather face a hundred demons than this path," Artyem grumbled.

"Don't say that word here, ever," Felix said seriously through his nasal voice.

"What? Does it summon them?" Artyem said sarcastically.

"In here it does," Felix said. Artyem said nothing. Emya thought the Companion might draw more demons and monsters than a word, but she didn't say it out loud in case referring to the object would help the demons along.

For at least an hour they trekked through the horrid tunnel. Emya was starting to think they would never get through it. Even if they did, being attached to the Companion and all it entailed was nowhere near as bad as the stinking tunnel. And if it was only going to get worse from here, they might as well turn back. Then the faintest rays of light permeated the darkness. Before long, a small opening, barely enough for a scrawny thing like Emya to squeeze through, appeared between the trunks. Felix and Artyem were both tall, though Felix was the less brawny of the two. Felix squeezed through with some effort. Emya followed and easily slipped through the opening. She did not see how Artyem squeezed through, though she was vaguely aware of some grunting and mumbled cursing.

The world had gone hazy. She rubbed her eyes, thinking the darkness had affected them somehow. But when she opened them, she saw that the haze had not gone. It was still hot, but at least not as hot as the tunnel. High in the sky, the sun was nothing more than an orange disk obscured by the shimmering haze and the wisps of purplish-gray clouds.

It was a desert wasteland. Soft sand, bare except for a scattering of short, gray tufts of grass, slipped under her shoes. A few short trees, twisted and mangled into knots, dotted the distant landscape.

"Let's get away from this smell," Felix said with disgust. Emya couldn't see how, as they were all covered in the stinking puss until Felix waved his hands and cleared it from their clothes.

Emya peered down at her dress in surprise. It was as though she had forgotten they were mages.

"I thought there would be more cover," Artyem said, his voice low.

"It wouldn't matter," Felix said. "The things in here can go through brush and stone. At least this way we'll see them coming."

"Then let's not waste time standing here presenting an easy target," Artyem said as he took the lead, striding confidently towards the north.

"If the... things in here can get us through solid stone, how are we going to rest?" Emya asked.

Felix took out the map they had copied from the library. "There is supposed to be a village on our path. If it's still there, we should be able to make it by nightfall. There are some accounts that the houses are made from magic-resistant materials, and I should be able to create a barrier within one that will protect us."

"That will keep us safe?" Emya asked,

"That will keep the creatures out," Artyem said darkly. "We are never safe here. Remember that."

Artyem's ominous aphorism proved to be true sooner than Emya expected. Scarcely five minutes had passed when a yellowish-gray creature, no taller than Emya's waist, emerged from the sand and loped towards them. Its bright, glowing yellow eyes fixed on Felix. It held its claws before it, reaching towards them, gurgling and frothing through its jagged, black teeth. The group stopped. Felix held up his hand, magic crackling between his fingers. Artyem drew two knives.

"What is that?" Emya asked.

"Emya, get ready to put up a shield if it comes for you," Felix said. "The things in here don't have names. Don't go wasting your energy thinking them up."

"I wasn't going to," Emya said defensively as she tried to recall what he'd taught her. Now all she could think of were names. Knife Fingers, Razor Teeth, Ugly Goblin Thing. The creature leaped at Felix with a strangled cry. Felix sent a bolt of magic straight into its eyes, knocking it back. Artyem stepped in and slashed a knife down its shoulder and out its ribs. Its arm fell off in a waterfall of yellow blood. His other knife cut through the creature's neck, its head hitting the sand with a soft thump. But the body pressed on, stumbling towards Felix, its last arm reaching for him. Felix shot a jet of flame that engulfed the body in a fire spout that shot up into the hazy sky. The creature collapsed and was still.

"Very flammable," Atryem said. "Warn me next time you're about to do that. I think you singed my eyebrows."

"Sorry," Felix said sheepishly. "They didn't do that last time I was here."

As they continued, Emya silently hoped that creature was the only one they would face but was quickly disappointed. The Ugly Goblin Things seemed to sprout out of the sand like daffodils in the spring. Artyem immobilized them, slashing off their legs, and then Felix burnt them to ash as they attempted to crawl towards the group. Quickly, these attacks drained the pair of energy and strength. There were no nice quiet picnics in the shade. At one point, when the creatures were far enough away, Felix grumpily slung his pack around to his front, dug around in it with one hand,

and pulled out part of a loaf of bread. He stuffed it in his mouth like a small child with a sweet treat and chewed quickly. Emya hadn't even noticed she was hungry until then but realized they wouldn't be able to stop and eat. She and Artyem followed Felix's lead. That was how they ate the rest of the day.

As the sun sank in the sky, the waning light seemed to energize the goblins. They clawed and bit Artyem as he struck. Felix was breathing heavily and had resorted to short bursts of flame that allowed the creatures to get dangerously close to him.

Emya struggled to call up the shield and holding it for too long was draining not just her magic but her will to fight. As one goblin was clawing at the sparking magic between them, she glanced at Felix, who shot a burst of flame at one on his left that fell short of the creature. Emya caught sight of one coming up on his back. Without thinking, she summoned a tongue of flame and shot it at the creature. Too late did she remember Felix telling her not to try to attack from behind a shield, as the magic would bounce back and hit her, just as if she was holding a piece of metal. A moment of panic was instantly replaced by surprise as the jet of fire went through the shield with a crackle and hit the goblin in its gnarled foot. The flash of heat caused Felix to stumble. Artyem caught notice of her then and sliced the goblin still attacking her shield. Felix finished it off with a spark. Emya moved away from the burning creature and let her shield down.

They were alone for a moment, or at least the goblins were far enough away that they could ignore them for a few minutes.

"How did I do that?" Emya said.

"You're control of fire is much stronger than you're shield. I'm surprised you didn't destroy it entirely," Felix said with pride in his voice.

"Then why am I using a shield? Why don't I help you fight?"

"You almost lit me on fire!"

"Just because you know how to use a weapon," Artyem interjected patiently, "does not mean you know how to fight."

"There's a difference?" Emya said tersely.

"Indeed, especially when fighting as a team," then he added to Felix, "we're not going to make it to cover in time. Why don't you create a shield around us all?"

"Because keeping a shield around a moving target is much harder than spraying a little fire. Though you're right, we must move faster."

"I think," Felix said after a few moments of walking in silence. "Despite her lack of training, we would move faster if Emya took on a more offensive role."

"Agreed," Artyem said, then he turned to Emya. "Just don't let them get too close or you're as likely to fry us as them."

"I know," Emya said with a hint of annoyance. "I saw

what happens when they catch fire."

"She's got you there Tyem."

This was easier said than done. Several close calls had both the men shooting her frightened and indignant looks. Yet they *were* moving faster now.

After a while, as the sun went down, the attacks became fewer and fewer.

"Maybe they go back into hiding when the powerful creatures come out at night," Felix suggested, squinting into the setting sun. The goblins seemed to be getting further away.

"Maybe they're tired of getting killed," Artyem said.

"We're not killing them," Felix said. "Just slowing them down."

Disturbed by that realization, Emya glanced over her shoulder to see if the stinking forest was still visible. She found it comforting to see a means of escape if things became too dire. The further away they got, the more nervous she became. To her surprise, the trees were gone, replaced by a mass of dark, purple puffy clouds.

"I think a storm is coming," she said. The clouds were moving towards them at an alarming rate.

"A new experience," Felix said, looking back over his shoulder. "This should be interesting."

Lightning streaked across the sky. A muted rumble of thunder followed.

"If those creatures are fleeing from the storm,"

Artyem said sagely, "ought we as well?"

He took Emya by the hand and started running, Felix at their heels. The storm was nearly overhead by the time the outline of a village appeared in the distance. Hot gusts of wind attempted to blow them over, but Artyem kept up a steady and exhausting pace. Emya sucked in breath after hot, painful breath as her calves burned in protest. Thunder boomed and lightning struck the ground ahead of them. They all jumped and halted in fright, though Artyem had them moving again almost instantly.

A harsh, metallic smell filled the air as they reached the abandoned village. Drops of something wet, sticky, and purple burned Emya's face and hands. Felix urged them into the nearest structure, a one-room house with a roof that pinged like metal as the rain began to pound it. The stone walls had no windows. The only opening to the outside besides the door was a small fireplace. The dirt floor was bare of furniture or any indication that anyone had ever lived there. It had been abandoned for a thousand years as far as Emya knew. Maybe everything else had turned to dust? The metallic smell overwhelmed the little room, but the sturdy construct kept the liquid at bay.

Emya wiped her hands and face clean on the back of her cloak and then handed it to Felix, who laid out all three and cleaned them instantly with magic.

"What is that stuff?" Emya asked, though too late

she realized Felix wouldn't know and probably didn't want to.

"Iron dissolved in acid, I think," he said to her surprise. "With raw magic as a catalyst."

"Will it dissolve the roof?" Emya asked.

"I don't think so. If anything here could destroy these buildings, it already would have."

"That makes sense," Artyem said.

"Yes, it does. Pity, it's only my best guess."

On that unsettling note, Emya's feet gave out and she fell on her clean cloak. She curled up on her side, her eyes closing, the patter of rain lulling her to sleep in moments.

~~*~*~*~*

All too soon, someone was gently shaking her awake. It took a little while before she could open her eyes. Felix was peering down at her, silhouetted in the light of a small fire.

"Are you hungry?" he asked.

Emya sat up and took a toasted cheese sandwich and a handful of dried fruit. Emya ate in silence, focusing on chewing. The storm hadn't let up. Felix sat down next to her and then laid back with his hands behind his head. Emya looked around the room. Artyem was wrapped in his cloak near the fire.

"Are you taking the first watch?" Emya asked.

"Yes. Turns out, when I'm back to full power and dragging us through a magical wasteland, he is more agreeable to the watch system."

"Should I take a watch?" Emya asked.

"Maybe later," Felix said. "You couldn't stay awake for more than a few minutes once we stopped."

As Emya finished her meal she watched Felix's eyes droop closed.

"Look who's talking," she murmured.

Emya debated whether she should wake Felix or stay up and keep watch herself. She was spared the decision when a loud crash of thunder jolted Felix out of his sleep. He sat up looking blearily around.

"Sorry," he said. "Was I out long?"

"No," Emya reassured him.

Felix sighed and shook his head, "this is not going to get any easier."

"I know. You've mentioned that," Emya said giving him a curious look.

"This place can change you. The constant stress, attacks, the magic messing with your head."

"And there's no guarantee we'll find what we're looking for," Emya added.

"Yeah."

"We're not going to be the same after this then."

"I don't know about that. Our magic does protect us and can heal us. If my magic had not been restored, I'm not sure I could have ever felt like myself again after what the Kings did to me."

"If it wasn't for your magic, they wouldn't have done anything to you."

"True." He patted her back appreciatively. "Why don't you go back to sleep?"

With a well-timed yawn, Emya agreed and laid back next to Felix and wrapped herself up in the cloak.

Chapter Five

Emya had scarcely drifted into sleep when a loud, shrill screeching woke her. She sat up, clutching her cloak to her chin. The screeching transformed into a loud, distressed wailing.

"Demons," Felix whispered beside her. Artyem was on his feet, blades drawn, facing the door.

"Can he fight them with blades?" Emya whispered as she got to her feet. Felix stood in front of her.

"I don't know," he said. "and I fear we are about to find out."

"These are forged from steel and bluestone ore," Artyem said. Emya was about to ask how that could affect the demons, but a loud screech and bang on the door stopped the words in her throat. She clutched

Felix's arm, watching the door with wide-eyed fear.

"Get ready to summon a shield," Felix murmured, peeling her off his arm.

Summoning her courage first, she took a few steps back from Felix to give him room to sling magic. The creature was now scratching at the sides of the little hut.

"Why can't it get in?" Emya asked.

"Old, strong magic from the wars," Felix said. "I don't understand it, but I sensed it as I wove protective magic."

The door rattled violently.

"It's diminishing the protective enchantments," Felix said as a heavy thump knocked the door off its hinges. Something enormous, dark, and putrid like rotting meat pushed through the narrow space. Frigid cold filled the little room. Emya stumbled back away from Felix. She barely summoned a shield as the creature's shadowy arm extended toward her. A blast of heat broke her shield almost instantly, engulfing her in a constricting grip of darkness. She struggled to draw breath as she was lifted off the ground. Suddenly, she hit the ground with a hard thump, though the vice-like grip did not release. She was lifted once more and hurled back down. Pain shot through her. This time the darkness relented, leaving her sprawled on the floor. Dazed, she lay on her back with eyes wide. The only light was from the stars in her vision bursting above her.

"Emya!" a soft voice called from far away, "Emya!"

The voice was getting louder and clearer. It called her name again and a soft light appeared among the stars. Emya blinked, her vision cleared and the ringing in her ears subsided. Felix peered down at her, his concerned features barely visible in the soft light of the tongue of fire in his hand.

"Emya, can you hear me?" he said, his voice still muted.

"Yes," she said with difficulty.

"Good," he said, relieved. "I'm going to keep healing you okay? Just relax."

Emya shut her eyes. A gentle tingle slowly filled her head. In a few moments, it was gone. It moved through her, settling on her aching limbs until the pain subsided.

"How's that?" Felix's voice was much clearer.

Emya sat up. "Much better. Good as new."

Felix grinned. "Good, I was worried that my healing skills had faded."

"What happened?" Emya asked, looking around. Artyem stood by the door hanging from a hinge.

"I tried to expel the demon with magic, but it was too strong. Artyem cut through its limb, releasing you and weakening it enough for me to banish it. We're very lucky."

"Luck had nothing to do with it," Artyem said. "My blades have magic resistive properties."

"And it turns out that it can harm demons," Felix said. "Something to add to the archives when we return."

If we return, the quiet voice inside Emya whispered. She ignored it.

"I didn't come out unscathed," Artyem said, turning towards them enough for Emya to see he was holding his arm, though he still had a blade in his injured hand.

"Let me see what I can do about it," Felix said.

"Later, I can still fight with it. If she is healed, then we must find shelter. This night is far from over."

Felix pulled Emya to her feet. They gathered their packs and cloaks and stepped out into the dark. If the Twisted Realm was strange during the day, at night it was absolutely bizarre.

The sky was a deep, luminous purple, with strange lights streaking, floating, and dancing across it. In contrast, the sand shimmered a dark, blood red. Chirping and buzzing insect-like creatures scuttled over the desert, either in search of food or fighting not to become food. One scampered onto Emya's foot. She kicked it off with a tiny, alarmed squeak.

Felix shushed her, though she questioned the necessity of silence. Noise filled the night, rushing sounds like wind, cracking like thunder, gurgling noises that sounded like nothing she'd ever heard. As they trod carefully through the village, shadows lurked around every corner, watching as they passed. Some reached out long limbs, but when Felix cast bright magic at them, they retreated.

"Why aren't they attacking us?" Emya whispered.

"They are," Felix said through gritted teeth. "I am keeping them at bay as best I can, but we must find shelter."

Artyem led them deep into the village until they came to a small, stone building barely larger than a storage shed.

"Stop," Felix said. Artyem halted, looking over his shoulder, his brow quizzical in the fuchsia light.

"They must have stored some magical item in here," Felix said. "It already has strong protection."

Artyem nodded and led them through another heavy door.

The floor was strewn with brittle rocks that cracked under their feet.

"Or some magical creature," Artyem said.

It took a moment for Emya to realize it was not brittle rocks, but brittle bones that they were stepping on.

"Disgusting," she murmured.

"No matter," Felix said. A gentle tingling buzzed through the air. Emya took a few steps around to discover, as she suspected, that Felix had banished the bones. A pleasant odor lingered.

"Nice touch," Artyem said.

They dropped their packs. Emya curled up in her cloak. Exhausted and jittery, she wondered if she would be able to sleep at all. One of the two men lay near her.

"Wake me if this shack collapses," Artyem said from

her side. Felix hummed in tired agreement.

"I didn't think I slept so long," Emya said. "Or did Felix insist on taking your watch?"

"No, you slept," Artyem said. "Though the nights here are far longer than the days, so you may not need to sleep much longer."

Emya couldn't sleep at all. After a long, agitated attempt to drift off, she sat up and crept over to where she sensed Felix.

"I'm right here," he suddenly whispered. "Don't step on me."

"Sorry." Emya sat, her knee brushing his. She wasn't sure if she was beside him or facing him.

"Maybe someday I'll be able to take a watch," she said.

"That would be nice," he sighed She could hear the smile in his voice. "But enjoy your sleep while it lasts."

"I wish I could right now," she said aggravated. "I can't settle down again."

"This is not an easy place to sleep. How are you feeling? Any headache or dizziness?"

Emya took a moment to think about this. Her head hurt, but she hadn't noticed until then. She felt a little unsteady, but that could have been from stress and exhaustion. Overall, she didn't feel too bad considering she'd had her head bashed against the floor within the hour.

"My head hurts a little. I'm tired and my nerves are

shot. I'm surprised I wasn't more seriously injured."

"It was too small a space for it to get much of a swing, thankfully."

Emya was still trying to accept that such a large creature existed even though she had experienced it firsthand.

"I might not be so lucky next time," she lamented. "I don't know how we can get through this."

"Truthfully, neither do I," Felix admitted. "We'll follow our map and our plan and hope for the best."

"If we do manage to survive--"

"We will," Felix interrupted.

"Once we're free," Emya went on, "what will we do?"

"Whatever we want," Felix said with the most cheer she'd heard from him in a while.

"No," Emya said. "I mean..."

Even just thinking about saying what she wanted to tell him made her even more nervous than facing the terrors of the Twisted Realm. Still, she hoped it would give her something to fight for. Something more than seeing Evris again, or learning magic in Civim.

"What will you and I do?"

Felix was silent for a moment. She hoped he understood. She didn't want to risk waking Artyem trying to put these feelings into words.

"If you want," he said slowly, "we can find out what it's like to be together without a magical object affecting our feelings for each other."

"Is that what you want?" she whispered so low she wasn't sure he could hear it.

"Yes," he said decidedly. "Though I would also like to know what it's like to be apart without worrying we might cause the other to pass out and die."

Emya smiled at the humor in his tone.

"That's something we have to look forward to then," she said.

She felt his hand brush her knee, then arm before finding her own. He took her hand in his and squeezed it gently and did not let go as they sat in silence, listening to the sounds of the night. As horrible as the screeching, whistling, and gurgling was, Emya slumped against him and diffed off into a dreamless sleep.

~~*~*~*~*

Shuffling and muffled whispers woke Emya. Though she felt as though she had slept a long time, the darkness of the room disoriented her.

"Is it morning?" she asked, her voice too loud in her ears.

"Yes," Felix said at a normal volume, the whispering no longer necessary now that she was awake, she supposed.

"Can we light a fire or something?" Emya asked. She was craving something hot to eat and the little hut was cooler than the outside.

"Not in here," Felix said. "It's too small and there isn't enough ventilation."

"Is there no way to make a little light?" she asked irritably, unsure of where her pack was and, though the room was small, she didn't feel like crawling along the dirty floor to find it.

"That's a good idea," Artyem said.

"Right," Felix said, and a moment later he was illuminated by a tiny ball of light.

"How do I make that?" Emya asked, mesmerized by the trick. She found the outline of her pack a few feet away.

"It's rather complicated," Felix said. "Light is one of the most difficult kinds of elemental magic. We understand so little about it. We often have to use the ancient language to manipulate it."

"I didn't hear you say anything," Emya said, digging in her pack for her dried fruit.

"Not out loud," he said.

"Maybe I could do it the way the Kings taught me."

"Try," Felix said to her surprise.

Emya held out her hand. She imagined a ball of light forming in it just like Felix's. She summoned her magic inside her, yet the light would not appear.

"I can't," she said, frustrated.

"That's because you don't understand what light is or how it works," Felix said.

"But I don't know how fire works either and yet I

can summon it."

"But you do know how fire works. You know it burns away wood and turns it to ash. You know water can put it out, and that certain things don't burn easily or at all. What do you know about light except that you can see it?"

Emya pondered this while she chewed on a handful of dried apple pieces.

"Nothing else I guess," she admitted.

"Exactly, neither do I. And yet we stand illuminated in this desolated place, scared by the magic that was used to create the ancient words with which I summoned pure light."

The light winked out.

"Oh," he said in surprise. "Well, even I'm not very good at light magic."

"Thanks for the magic lesson," Artyem said. "If you're ready, we should move on. I don't care to hear any more about the people who destroyed this place until we get out of it."

Emya stuffed some bread into her mouth and washed it down with a gulp of water before pulling her pack over her shoulder. When all were ready Artyem slowly opened the door, peered around outside, and gestured for them to follow. Emya quickly stepped behind Felix as the light and heat flooded the little room. Felix reached back and grabbed her hand, squeezing it gently before letting go and following Artyem out into the dim morning.

The sky was pale lavender and the sand had become sparkling orange. Emya was growing tired of the unnatural colors. Everything about the Twisted Realm grated at her nerves. Artyem set a brisk pace as he led them along the village's twisting paths. If there were ever paved roads, they were long since buried in sand or perhaps disintegrated. They slipped and slid through the sand until they emerged from the village at the base of a range of rocky hills. The terrain at least had mercifully become firm clay. Massive boulders dotted the hills; some so precariously perched that Emya feared they would topple onto the trio.

Felix looked pleased at least.

"We must climb these hills?" Emya asked incredulously. As if the desert hadn't been trying enough.

"Yes, we're going the right way," Felix said.

Emya sighed and trekked forward resolutely. She wasn't sure she would have the energy to summon a shield for long. Yet, after half a day of climbing, she had spotted none of the Goblins or any other creature. Perhaps they didn't care for the difficult terrain?

"Are we going to find another town to stay in?" Emya asked as they rested for a bit, standing in the shade of a particularly large boulder, though it made little difference in the temperature.

"There is no village on our path," Artyem said. "We

will have to make our own shelter."

"That's not strictly true," Felix said. Artyem shot him a look over his shoulder. "She already knows about the inhabited villages," he added defensively.

"We're not going near any of those, so we need not bring it up."

"You don't like talking about dangerous things do you, Artyem?" Emya said, becoming tired of his closed-mouth policy.

"It's not that," Felix said. "Artyem is very superstitious."

"I am not," Artyem said indignantly.

"Yes, you are. You believe speaking of things may cause them to come to pass."

"I do not," Artyem insisted. "I believe words have power, and words that deal with magic doubly so."

"That's not how magic works. It's still a superstition."

"There are magic words. That's what the ancient language is."

"Yes, but it is not the words that have power, it is the mage."

"When I was little, my parents told me not to speak to anyone but them because my words might do magic," Emya cut in. "I think they just told me that to keep me from talking to people about magic. When I was that little I didn't understand how people felt about me."

Artyem gave her a sympathetic look but said nothing else. Felix looked as though he wanted to say something but let the subject close. It was time to move on anyway.

The day seemed to pass quickly, though Emya thought the long harrowing night had skewed her perception. They did not stop again, and though Emya did not want to waste any more time, she was very sore and tired. Her head throbbed despite all Felix had done to mend it. She knew that the pain was from injury and not just the strain of the journey. She had never experienced shooting pains through her head as she did then. She wanted so badly to rest. Casting thoughts of the pain aside she distracted herself with more pleasant thoughts of her conversation with Felix the night before. Felix hadn't tried to hold her hand the entire day. Did he not want Artyem to see? Or were her feelings stronger than his? Maybe he just wanted his hands free in case they were attacked. She sighed dejectedly at her pleasant thoughts turning to unnecessary worry. Whatever Felix thought of her fluctuating emotions, he kept to himself.

As the day grew dim and they reached the top of a particularly high hill, Emya saw what Artyem had not wanted to discuss. A very reasonably short distance away was another village, and this one did not look deserted. Smoke rose from the chimneys. There was movement between the houses, and the smell of cooking wafted over the air.

Emya opened her mouth to say something but

was met with a shush. To her surprise, it hadn't come from Artyem. They hurried down the hill into the cover of some large, jagged rocks. The rocks formed a small shelter which Artyem led them into before mercifully stopping.

"We can talk now," Felix said, "but keep your voice low."

"Do the inhabitants ever come in here?" Artyem asked.

"I don't think so," Felix said. "Not enough raw magic here. It could kill them."

"They can't survive without raw magic?" Emya asked in surprise. "I thought raw magic was dangerous?"

"Nothing in here can live without it. The creatures feed off it. The people who have lived here all these centuries have become dependent on it as well."

"It doesn't drive them mad?"

"They are mad, but I don't know if the magic drives all reason from them or if they have been raised to behave like animals because that was all their ancestors knew. Either way, we must stay away from them."

"Why isn't there as much raw magic here?" Emya asked. She hadn't noticed until then that she felt less anxious. and it didn't smell as bad. As the sun went down the air had cooled.

"Tritium rock," Felix said, tapping the wall.

"How did rock from the Tritium mountains get here?" she asked.

"It's not from the Tritium mountains. It can be found all over the world. We just call it Tritium rock because that's where we get it."

They pulled food from their packs and had the most pleasant meal they'd ever had in the Twisted Realm. Emya sat next to Felix, and Artyem across from them. Something about him drew her gaze. He looked... distressed. Emya didn't know him very well despite all the time they spent together. She had only really talked to him about herself or Felix.

"What's the matter, Artyem?" Emya asked gently.

Artyem's gaze rose slowly from his lap.

"Nothing," he said lightly.

"Is it the villagers?" she persisted.

"No," he said.

Emya frowned and glanced at Felix. By now she would have expected him to cut in with some quick remark or joke to end the subject, thus sparing his friend, or he would simply say what he knew was bothering Artyem. Instead, his head was bowed as he purposefully avoided either of their gazes. It was left to Emya to either drop the subject or pursue it, and perhaps Felix wanted her to because Artyem would shut down the topic if Felix tried to get involved.

Emya chose her next words carefully, as she believed words were the problem.

"I've been thinking about what you said, about words having magical power."

"Oh?" he said with mild interest.

"Well, I was wondering how you came to believe that."

A mixture of emotions filled his expression. At first, it seemed he might not answer, though it looked like he wanted to. The few moments that passed seemed an eternity. Finally, he let out a heavy sigh.

"When I was a child," he started slowly, "about seven, I had a fight with my father. I don't remember what it was about, but I raged and ran about the house and threw things. Finally, he picked me up, put me in my room, and locked the door. I became so angry. Angrier than I had ever been in my short life, or ever was after. I screamed at him, 'I want you to die tonight.' He didn't say another word. The next morning, he was dead." Artyem bowed his head, his face becoming red.

"And you think your words killed him?" Emya asked gently. She glanced at Felix, expecting him to jump in and assure his friend he hadn't, but Felix was also looking at the ground.

"That night, when my rage subsided and I fell into an exhausted sleep I had a dream," Artyem said. "A dream that magic burst from me in the form of a strong man that went into my parents' room and strangled my father. My mother was away that night. She came home early in the morning and found him dead, strangled in his bed. I told her what I had dreamed, and she took me straight to Civim, to the Masters. No one knew I could do magic. They tested me and checked my father. They said there was no doubt my first act of magic had killed my father."

Emya stared at him in horror. Deep within her, something stirred. Something she had long repressed.

"You can do magic?" she asked, too shocked to weigh her words.

"Not anymore," Felix said softly. "He's refused to use it since that day. It's dried up now."

"I couldn't stop my magic," Artyem continued flatly, "but I know if I hadn't said those words out loud, my magic wouldn't have killed him."

"You felt that way," Felix said with intense sympathy. "Your feelings, uncontrolled in such a young boy, are what directed your magic that night."

"I know what I felt," Artyem said. "I know those words had more control over my magic than I did. I could feel it as my magic was strangling him. The magic figure said them out loud over and over."

Artyem quickly dropped his head as his voice broke. Tears fell silently on the dusty rock.

"I'm so sorry," Emya said, hurrying over to Artyem. She wrapped her arms around him. He rested his head on her shoulder. After a few moments, he broke away, wiping his eyes and taking a deep breath.

"I have to tell you something though," Emya said. "I dreamed my magic killed my parents the night they died."

They both gave her surprised looks.

"I dreamed it killed a lot of people," she went on, "but the night my parents died, I dreamed my magic seeped out of me and formed into a shadow person. It crept into my living room and stabbed my parents to death with a blade of nothing. The next morning, I found them dead exactly as they lay in my dream."

"Emya you did not kill your parents, Azo did," Felix said sharply.

"What?" Emya said in shock. "How do you know?"

"Because Azo went into the village that night to scout out for their 'invasion' and your father caught him. Azo sweet-talked him and your father invited him to stay at your house. He bragged to Fen about how he had slaughtered them both."

"Why didn't you tell me?" Emya breathed, and a mixture of anger, confusion, and pain welled up inside her. Why would he have kept something so important from her?

"I couldn't bring myself to," Felix said, wincing as her pain struck him. "You had so much to deal with and I was so weak for so long. I meant to find time to tell you, but a good moment never presented itself. I should have told you and I'm sorry."

Emya's anger ebbed. They had certainly been busy. She couldn't think of a good moment when she would have wanted him to tell her either.

"Is that what the councilors were hiding from me?"

she asked, aching for a little more revelation in the mystery of her parent's death, "Is that the real reason they wouldn't let me in the house?"

"I don't think so," he said. "I couldn't tell you for sure as Azo said nothing more about it."

Emya sighed with some relief. She had tried to believe their deaths weren't her fault, even though she believed it so. Now that she knew, she felt lighter. And awkward. She suddenly wished she hadn't brought it up right after Artyem had told her something so personal.

"I'm so sorry," she said again to Artyem. "I understand why you don't like magic very much."

Artyem nodded stoically. She couldn't tell if talking to her had helped him feel better, but at least his countenance returned to his old self.

"Well, since you both have told a story, I guess it's my turn," Felix said, though Emya could tell he was trying to bring the atmosphere back to normal conversation. "How about the time I fell into a beehive on the farming ring?"

Artyem snorted. It wasn't much of a story in Emya's opinion. All that happened was he tried to create a gentle stream of water and the blast of water he produced knocked him back into the beehive. Still, it made Artyem smile.

~~*~*~*~*

Emya was grateful for the quiet night. The rocks didn't glow and only a dim light from the glowing night sky illuminated their shelter. Felix still cast protective magic, and Artyem took the first watch. Emya was surprised to be shaken awake by Felix before dawn. It seemed the journey was taking its toll on him and Artyem. Both had agreed to wake her for a short watch at the end of the long night. Emya sat watching the glow of the sky fade as the sun rose, happy to be taking some of the burden of the watch from her two protectors.

The two woke shortly after sunrise. While they ate breakfast Artyem pulled out the map and explained the next part of the journey.

"I hope you both enjoyed being dry. Our path from here takes us into a swamp," Artyem said. "The Fortress is hidden somewhere around there." He pointed to a large circle drawn in a larger area labeled 'nasty, disgusting swamp.' She doubted that was the original labeling.

"And the swamp is hidden with magic," Felix said. "Scholars have theorized that an undetectable concealing barrier is generated by a powerful magical object within."

"Then how will we find it?" Emya asked wryly.

"Magic," Felix said.

"Of course."

"Hear me out," Felix continued. "I've been studying barrier magic. It's one of my projects and one of the reasons I've had to come here."

"So, Felix is going to try to detect the barrier,"

Artyem continued, "and assuming he can do that, break through it, and find the fortress."

"And if he can't?" Emya asked.

"Then we go home," Artyem said. "But before we get to the barrier, there are a few other things we have to look out for. Number one is the monstrous creature that might be within or near the barrier. Magic traps, deadly pockets of concentrated raw magic, and who knows what other perils."

Emya's heart sank. She hadn't realized how ill-prepared they were for this endeavor. She knew the chance to break the Companion's hold was slim. It was possible this sorcerer hadn't even made the object. Maybe they should have searched the library some more before setting out.

"I'm certain I can do it," Felix said confidently. "And when I do, along with getting away from this wretched object, I will be able to write a book on magical barriers."

"They might even give you your own class," Artyem said, then added with a considerable degree of sarcasm, "is that the real reason you wanted to come here?"

"No," Felix said with a laugh. "But there isn't much of a chance we will find what we're looking for anyway, so at least I get something out of it."

"If we survive," Emya added darkly.

"Have courage," Felix said. "Think of this as the adventure of a lifetime. You'll find learning magic and making friends is easy compared to this."

Emya smiled and blushed. She wished she hadn't told him about her trouble with making friends.

"He's right," Artyem said, standing up. "Everyone will want to hear of your adventures. They'll all want to say they've met you."

"Those sound more like fans than friends," Emya said.

"Even better," Felix said.

They started walking down the rocky hill. Emya could see tall, mossy trees in the distance. The only warning that something was amiss was a soft scraping sound.

Artyem let out an agonized scream and Emya caught sight of a dark claw protruding from his leg. He was yanked off his feet and into the air as an enormous demon stood up from behind a large boulder.

"Artyem!" Felix yelled. The creature turned and loped down the hill. Felix shot off after it, throwing crackling balls of magic that were absorbed into its shadowy hide. Emya tried to keep up, but Felix was too fast. Soon she was far behind him. Not far enough to cause her to pass out, as Felix had the Companion, but far enough that Felix didn't notice a demon pluck her from the ground. Emya was enveloped in the darkness. She had some sense of being carried away, but her screams were silenced inside the shadow. She didn't know if it was her inability to breathe or distance from the Companion that drew her into senselessness, but her last thought was gratitude as the pain diminished.

Chapter Six

A short dream preceded Emya's awakening. It was simple, yet disturbing. In her mind, she saw an image of Azo striding down a narrow cavern tunnel, torch held aloft and illuminating his triumphant, twisted smile, paralyzing her with fear. Her eyes snapped open. Heart racing, pumping fear through her, she wanted to tell herself it was just a dream, but she knew there was a good possibility it wasn't. Scared as she was, it took her a moment to realize that, although her eyes were open, they might as well have been closed. It was pitch black. The hard, grating stone beneath her was wet with what she suspected was her blood. She ached all over and her right arm hurt so much she knew it was broken. There was no doubt that she was in a cave, and if Azo was somehow, somewhere nearby, she needed to escape before he found her.

Slowly sitting up, another grim realization struck her. Felix, unless the demon had overcome him and taken it, had the Companion and she had no idea where he was or what direction would knock her senseless again. At least, she comforted herself, being awake meant Felix might be close by.

Wishing she could conjure elemental light, she made do with a little flickering flame, the heat irritating her many injuries. Holding it in front of her, she could see nothing but the path below her feet. She shuffled forward tentatively. With nothing to feed the flame, she had to concentrate her magic to keep it burning. Even so, her magic didn't keep the flame lit the same way an oil-soaked torch would, and soon the flame winked out. It was more difficult each time she brought the flame back. There were matches in her pack, though she had no idea where it was. No matter. Matches didn't burn long either.

She hadn't gone far before she could no longer summon the flame. Exhausted and despairing, she was on the verge of panic. Shuffling along, eventually, her toes touched a vertical surface. Stretching out her good arm, she confirmed it was a wall.

Emya moved slowly, keeping her good hand on the wall, and carefully feeling with each step, as the wall might continue while the floor ended. After a while, she came to another wall, and then another after that. Huffing in frustration, she hoped she would find a pathway soon and that she wasn't trapped, as she feared she was. The demon could have climbed down with her into a pit only it could climb out of. Just as she was about to panic again, she found a jagged corner that went sharply in a different direction. A quick inspection indicated it was a passage.

As she moved down the passage it became incredibly difficult to squeeze through the narrow parts. As it grew smaller and smaller, she was beginning to question why she had left the cavern at all. Facing the demon again was starting to seem no more perilous than this directionless flight. Then she turned a corner and her heart soared. Light, dim but beautiful, illuminated a small opening. Emya could barely squeeze through it but once she did, she found herself in a large cavern open to the sky.

The glowing night filled the small cavern. At first Emya was dismayed. There was no apparent passage along the circular walls. Then, with a slower glance around, she found a patch of wall that was slightly darker than the area around it. It was a narrow passage much like the one she had just emerged from. Emya took a deep breath and turned back to the cavern. She needed to think and rest before attempting another passage.

She was still conscious, which was promising.

And, unless someone had taken the Companion from Felix, she must have been near both. Maybe he was somewhere in the cavern. Perhaps, even, the demon was with him. How long until it came in search of her?

She was starving too. Her stomach growled and twisted into angry knots. Trying to ignore her hunger, Emya took a deep breath and turned to continue through the passage when movement across the cavern caught her eye. Something that she had mistaken for a rock in the shadows was now getting to its feet.

Emya froze. Had she just woken some slumbering monster? As it straightened up, she realized it was a man. She didn't find much comfort in that fact, and she made no motion or sound. He looked around the cave and settled his gaze on her. He stepped towards her with a hobbled sort of gait. When he stepped out of the shadow, the dim glow of the night sky illuminated the horror concealed by the dark. It wasn't a person, it was a corpse.

Emya had heard tales of the corpses of the undead attacking her village and the mighty warriors that had fought them off, but she had never really believed them. Except for a strange young man who was desperate for water, she had never seen anything that resembled a reanimated corpse.

It staggered towards her, its flesh hanging in jagged chunks off its bones. Its lidless eyes, loose in their sockets, swirled around in its head. Emya turned and pushed her way into the passage. To her intense relief, the narrow passage was short and let out into a larger path. She hurried forward; her arms held out in front of her. There was no time to feel around with her feet as the relentless shuffle of the corpse pursued her faster than she thought possible.

As she turned a corner, she saw a light shining from around another corner, the sight of it bringing sweet relief. She ran for it as fast as she could. Something tangled underfoot and sent her sprawling. Her chin hit the stone hard, and she bit her tongue. Blood filled her mouth. She spat it out, pushing herself up gingerly on her bleeding, scraped-up hands.

Gazing around frantically for what had tripped her, she saw a rotting hand close around a fistful of her dress. With a screech of terror, she pulled frantically at her clothes. She stood up and used her weight to pull away, but the corpse possessed inhuman strength. Another hand grabbed her hair. She screamed in terror and pain as the corpse slowly pulled her back into the cave. Emya never imagined that her worst nightmare would be the end of her in this twisted realm. After everything she put up with, everything she did, everything she survived— the death of her parents, Kamala's vicious guardianship, the Kings' manipulations— she had survived it all and saved Felix. Now she was going to die at the rancid hands of a monster she had believed to be nothing more than a tale to scare her.

Emya howled a long, desperate, wail from deep within her. Magic, fueled by anger and fear, burst from within her and took the form of glittering gold chains that wrapped around the two corpses, paralyzing them and dragging them to the wall and securing them there. Emya, shaking, bloodied, and free, stared at the sight for just a moment before striding quickly away. Magic was a strange and fickle thing, she decided. The magic that conjured the chains was no longer connected with her, and she had no idea how long it would last. She turned the corner of the passage and found herself in a narrower tunnel lit with torches on the wall. She hurried along and turned the corner into another lit tunnel, and then another. As she turned the next corner, she was met by the back of a large, monster of a man. She recognized him just as the rush of darkness swallowed her up.

Azo.

~~*~*~*~*

Emya's world blinked on. She was immediately aware of the burning and stinging on her tongue, hands, and knees. Her whole body ached with pain and fatigue. After a few moments, she became aware of the presence of another. With what energy she could muster, she turned her head to find Azo sitting cross-legged not three feet from her. Sensing movement, his gaze turned from the flickering torchlight to her. He smiled that awful, knowing smirk.

"Your magical prowess has improved," he said conversationally. "Did the bookworms teach you the words to conjure enchanted chains?"

"No," Emya said, easing into a sitting position. Azo watched with an amused expression. "How do you know about that?"

She was sure she hadn't seen him, but maybe he had watched her struggle with the undead.

"They are still restraining the dead." He gestured vaguely behind him. "After all this time, the spell is still working. It's even caught a few more of the pesky things."

"How long have I been out?" Emya asked, ignoring his praise.

"A few hours. It's nearly dawn."

Emya sighed inwardly. The less time she spent passed out the better. It seemed to her that Felix, wherever he was, wasn't moving around too much. Then an upsetting idea struck her.

"Where is Gabak-Fen?" she snapped.

"My dear bother," Azo said. "He always has more brawn than brain. I'm afraid he was killed by our former magic vessel. Or what comes as close to death as he and I will ever experience."

Emya bristled at Felix being referred to as nothing more than a vessel, but she would not give Azo the satisfaction of getting under her skin.

"What do you mean?" Emya said, focusing on the

119

more important point. "When did Felix fight you?"

"It was he and I who attacked you outside those magic-draining rocks."

"You're saying you're a demon?"

"We call ourselves living shadows."

Emya interrupted him with a laughing snort. 'Living shadow' is what they had reduced Felix to. It was fitting they had been reduced to it themselves since they had lost the companion. But perhaps they had always been shadows. When she did not elaborate Azo went on. "'Demon' makes us sound as though we are evil monsters." He smiled at her. "We are evil monsters, but not because of what we've become."

Emya knew he wanted her to ask more so she stayed silent. She knew he wanted to tell her because it would scare her, so she needn't invite more fear into her already terrified heart.

"We were human once," he went on as though she'd asked. "We fought in the great wars of this land. We had magic like no other. Power beyond your imagination. We did things that would haunt your waking dreams. We won battle after battle for our sorcerer master, but at great cost. We became shadows, nothing more than darkness and magic. We had converted our human forms into power and death. We found we could not leave this sacred land. Only the scorching magic that ravages this place could sustain us. Soon we became aware of nothing but each other. Fen and I, all we ever

120

cared about was the other. I think that is why we had enough awareness to do something about it. These other shadows—you've met them, I'm sure—are nothing more than mindless forces of destruction now. Pity. I don't think they are aware of themselves enough to enjoy the death and disaster they cause. Fen and I found our old master's secret fortress. We slipped through the magical barrier like smoke. Inside, there was little left of our master's creation."

"But you found one," Emya said, barely containing her excitement.

"It found us," Azo said. "It tried to consume our essences and it nearly succeeded, but it must have been our awareness that spared us. I've told you the power of emotion in magic. We had to fight it for centuries, almost a thousand years. I don't think our master ever envisioned what happened to us. Little by little, particle by particle, we became ourselves; we formed our old bodies. We thought we were back to normal. Human again. So, we left, taking the object with us. As soon as we left the Twisted Realm we began to disintegrate. The object was not sustaining us as it had. We had to return to the realm, but we were so far away. We were almost discovered by someone who was traveling away from the realm. We hid in the trees, but the object slipped from my dissolving hand. And who should pick it up but a young mage?"

"Felix," Emya breathed.

"The object latched on to him and drained his magic. It nearly killed him. Luckily, I acted quickly and took the object. I took its gift of magic and restored Fen and myself to our full bodies, or so I thought. We kept the boy and the object and used it to give ourselves magic again, just as we had when our master gave us the magic to fight his dreadful war."

"Why didn't the object attach itself to you?" Emya asked.

"We never had magic of our own," Azo said. "And when we were shadows of ourselves, we had to fight to gain magic from it, enough to restore us. Only a true mage can form a connection with it, or so we believed. You were not the first we tried to replace that troublesome mage with. The others simply weren't as strong as you. The objects killed them the first time they made the connection."

Emya frowned at her lap. Felix hadn't mentioned that.

"He never told you, did he?" Azo said, astute as ever.

"No," Emya admitted. "But why should he? He didn't kill them, you did."

Azo shrugged. "I care not for the petty squabbles of you children anyhow."

"So, what happened after he and I left my village? Did you become demons again right away?" Emya didn't care to call him anything else. He was an evil demon as far as she was concerned. To her satisfaction, he frowned slightly.

"We had enough magic to travel back here, but we barely made it. Since we've returned, we could reform into our human bodies at will. As long as we have the power."

"But Fen is dead now. It's just you," Emya reminded him.

"Like I said, dead as much as we can be. Now only one question remains. What shall I do with you?"

"You can kill me," Emya said. "You're not getting the Companion."

"Is that what you call it?" Azo smiled. "I have a better idea. How about a trade?"

"I'm not trading you the Companion either," Emya said stubbornly. "Even if we can become free of it. Now that I know you'll just find another mage to entrap, I'll never let you have it. So just kill me."

"Hear me out, child," he said, a dangerous tinge in his tone. "If all I wanted was to take the object and your little mage friend, I could have done it by now. I had the opportunity. I took you alone for a reason."

"Because I couldn't defend myself. Felix and Artyem would have killed you."

"Perhaps. But I wouldn't have left them up to Fen if my goal was to capture the object."

Emya could believe that. Gabak-Fen lacked any kind of brains.

"I no longer wish to leave this place," Azo went on,

almost wistfully. "The world is so different now. People get upset when you take over their village."

"They didn't get upset before?"

"Not really. There was always the chance the new rulers would be better than the old. Magic is different now as well. It's not as powerful as it used to be. Even with the scraps of magic we tore out of your friend, we could have made crops grow across those grassy planes. We could have beckoned the rain."

"You could have taken that spell off my village before everyone went crazy."

"Indeed, although when you broke the spell they should have gotten better, not worse. There was another kind of magic there, one we could not control. I never understood it."

"Alright," Emya said. She was eager to be gone if there was a possibility of it. "If we find a way to sever the connection, and if we decide to give you the object, what's in it for us?"

"You never were the brightest student," Azo said. "I told you I know where my master's fortress is. I will show you and your friends the way. Once you are there, if you find some way to release yourselves from it, all you have to do is convince Felix to leave the object there. You can be rid of your burden and myself at once."

Liar, Emya thought, pursing her lips. Felix would never agree to leave the Companion for Azo to do as he pleased. Yet she was sure Azo expected them to double-cross him even if they said they would give it to him. On the other hand, if she didn't agree to his terms, she doubted she would be getting out of the cave alive. What choice did she have? One way or another, Azo would try to get what he wanted. If he had to kill her, Felix, and Artyem to do it, he would. The fact that he hadn't done just that was both worrying and comforting. They had some advantage over him, but she never knew Azo to see a disadvantage as anything less than a challenge.

"Okay," Emya said, taking a deep breath. "Lead me out of this cavern and show me where Felix and Artyem are. I shall relay your offer to them. If they agree, we shall meet you at the fortress and relinquish the Companion. If they don't agree, we shall meet you all the same. Prepare for a battle in that case."

Azo beamed with pride. "The Emya I met would never dare speak to me that way. You have certainly grown."

Emya wouldn't give him the satisfaction of admitting a guilty sense of gratitude at those words. He may have been telling her exactly how he felt, but it changed nothing. He would kill her all the same

~~*~*~*~*

The trek through the cave was not a pleasant one. Many of the passages were narrow, though Emya passed through them more easily than Azo. The undead kept up a relentless pursuit. Azo had power over them. He could slow them down but he did not have the magic Emya wielded. Though she was worn out, hungry, thirsty, and her power depleted, she was able to summon an impenetrable shield. Azo didn't seem to mind fighting them off with his bare hands.

The journey was long though, and Emya's shields were becoming weaker. Exhausted once more, she stopped in the middle of a large cavern.

"I don't suppose you have any food or water?" she asked irritably. Azo handed her a flask that hung from his waist. Emya took a swing and was pleasantly surprised to find it was crisp sweet water. She had expected it to be alcohol. Azo would find that kind of trick funny.

"Do demons need water?" Emya asked, pleased by the irritated twitch of his features at her continued use of the term.

"It is a habit preserved from my humanity, though unnecessary," he said. "Just as the desire to take human form."

"If you brought me here, where is my pack?" she asked. "I had water and food with me."

"It was lost as I was bringing you here. Perhaps you may come upon it on your way to find your friends."

"Do you really know where they are?"

"I have an idea," he said. "They were taken by the villagers."

Emya was a little shocked by the news. Both Felix

and Artyem had been wary of the people living in the Twisted Realm. She hoped their fears had not been realized.

"How do you know they're still there?" she asked, knowing her companions would have tried any means of escape, and had they failed, there was no point in her going to the village. No, she must not think like that.

"I don't, but what other choice do you have but to try and find them?"

"None, I suppose. How far is the village?" she asked. She didn't know how long she would last all alone with her magic depleted.

"From the cave mouth, it is not far at all. Perhaps half a day."

"I need to rest," she said, looking around for the smoothest spot to sit.

"We are almost out of here," he said irritably. Emya ignored him and sat. Feeling around to ensure that her spot was free of pebbles, she reclined on her side, pillowing her head with her hands.

"You're going to sleep in the presence of the enemy? I could just kill you."

"You could have killed me at any point," she said, refusing to be cowed by him the way she used to. "I need to rest if I am going to cross the realm by myself."

Azo relented and sat where he had been standing. Emya didn't know how long she slept, only that all her aches and pains woke her. Still exhausted, she could tell that her magic had returned somewhat. Blinking until her eyes adjusted to the low torchlight, she found Azo awake, staring at her.

"You were watching me sleep?" she asked. She was never that interesting to him before. He looked to be tired and in a foul mood.

"There is little else to look at," he said. "Are you ready?"

"Yes." Emya stood up, brushed the dust from her clothes, and straightened them. Azo led the way out of the cavern. He had not exaggerated when he said they were close. Emya estimated they had walked only ten minutes before daylight illuminated the cavern. They stopped at the mouth and looked around. Beyond the opening of the cave was a landscape that closely resembled a forest. Putrid bare black and brown trunks twisted around each other and were so dense that Emya couldn't see through them. Green, yellow, and black oozes seeped out, coating the ground. Emya looked at her shoes dubiously. They were already dirty, but she didn't want the goo to seep in.

"You won't be in here long, go straight that way," he pointed to the left, "until you emerge onto the desert. Then travel west along the forest until you see the village in the distance."

"And when are you going to tell me where the fortress is?"

Azo pointed to the right. "North through this forest

from the village. By the end of a day's travel from the village, you will come to a magic barrier. It can only be detected by a descendant of Pike, of which you and I are."

"And if you aren't?" she asked, not a little curious as to how he knew she was Pike's descendant.

"You would cross through the entire fortress with a single step. It is very impressive magic."

"And how do I get all of us through it?"

"You will know when you arrive."

Emya gave him a scathing look, but the small smirk on his face told her that he had said all he was going to. Without another word to him, she turned and strode off without a glance back. It was convenient that she seemed to be a descendant of the sorcerer who created the object Azo had attached her to. Had he known before he arrived? It now seemed impossible he had found her by accident.

Strolling quickly turned into struggling through the heavy growth. Thorny vines tore at her clothes and exposed skin. Whatever she couldn't break she had to either climb over or push past. Soon she was sweaty and out of breath, not to mention sticky from the plant secretions. What dim light seeped through the foliage was fading, and Emya found herself trapped in a tangle of vines with the clear desert visible beyond a hole in the foliage. Emya huffed, as she used simple magic to cut the vines around her.

When Emya had first been taught the different kinds of magic, she hadn't understood how magic could be different. It all seemed the same to her. Now she had a simple realization: It wasn't the magic that was different, it was the world around her that magic reacted to differently. The vines were living things, but they seemed to be made of stone-like material. She tried to pull the water from them but was unable to remove it from the tough outer flesh. Yet she could cut through the vines the same way she reshaped the blocks in her classes. At least she was learning something while she struggled.

It seemed as though, no matter how many vines she cut, there were ten more snaking around her. As she carefully sliced at several vines around her ankle, she saw with the burning of terror coursing through her that one of the vines moved on its own around her arm. It was pulling her hand away from her ankle so she could not direct the magic.

"A moving, thinking plant," she muttered. The plant had grown tired of her relentless attacks, it seemed, and was now trying to drag her back into the forest. It pulled her into the air and wrapped around her arms and legs. Emya squirmed helplessly. Up she went until she came face to face with... a face. It was a small round bulb at the end of a thin vine with protruding black eyes and a slit for a mouth. The slit opened and emitted a hissing sound.

"What are you?" Emya whispered. She hadn't expected it to reply.

"I am the being of all magic," it hissed.

Emya scoffed. "Is that so? What is such an important being doing in this silly forest?"

She spoke with much more confidence than she felt, but she would not be intimidated by a plant.

"I am the forest and the mountain. I am the minerals and the flesh. I am the being of all magic."

"What do you want?"

"To be released from this realm of twisted, dirty magic."

It either meant the strange vines, or the Twisted Realm, or perhaps both. Regardless, Emya would not help the creature.

"I don't know how," Emya said truthfully enough. "Let me go and I will find my friends. Perhaps they can help."

"They won't help me," it said. "You must release me."

"I won't help you either," she said defiantly. She struggled against the vines as they wrapped more tightly around her. The being watched patiently.

"Release me," it reiterated. Emya wondered why it wasn't threatening her, though perhaps the crushing vines were threat enough.

"No!" A surge of magic and anger coursed through her and she destroyed the vines around her all at once. She fell to the ground, which was mercifully cleared of the vines, but more were snaking towards her from above. She leaped to her feet and sprinted the short distance out of the forest of vines. Still, the being stretched after her. The thin tendrils tickled her arms as she barely outran their reach. With a glance over her shoulder, she saw the vines retreating into the forest. Emya turned back then wailed in frustration. Tall, dark shadows loomed before her. Screeching little monsters scampered in her direction, claws flailing. Intuitively she knew that a shield would not be enough, but she didn't have the power to fight all of the creatures.

As the first shadow approached, she shot a blast of air at it, but it blew right through the shadow without slowing the creature. Panting from the effort but still determined, she summoned a flame. It was small, not much bigger than her palm, but the shadows withdrew. The flailing creatures kept coming. Holding the fire in one hand, she blasted the creatures with wind as she ran across the desert. All that fueled her power was the raw desire to survive and find Felix and Artyem. It was almost dark now, but she could see the outline of a village and the magic repelling stones they had traveled through before she was taken. Emya blasted the last few creatures out of her way. Her path to the village was clear now as it rose before her. Then a gust of air blew out her dwindling fire. Within moments, a mass of shadow towered over her and enveloped her. The dark consumed her, filling her eyes, nose, mouth, and ears. It squeezed her from the outside and drowned her from the inside. With the last of her strength, she tried to summon fire but failed. Then she felt nothing.

Chapter Seven

Intense pain engulfed her awareness. Each breath was painful. There was a familiar sound that hurt her ears. Something touched her face and her skin burned.

Stop, Emya moaned in her thoughts, but she couldn't make her lips move. Let me die. But she didn't die, and as she slowly became aware of the world around her, the pain increased tenfold. When she thought it couldn't get any worse something was poured into her mouth that scalded her throat and burned in her stomach. Coughing with hot tears pouring down her cheeks, Emya's eyes opened. A dark, blurred shape loomed over her, silhouetted in the glowing purple sky. The burning coursed through her to the tips of her fingers and toes. Her screams of pain trapped in her throat.

Then, as suddenly as it had come on, the burning subsided, replaced by a cool calm. Her vision sharpened, and she focused on the shape hovering above her. It wasn't Felix or Artyem. Large dark eyes were set in stone gray skin. Strength coursed back into her muscles, and she sat up and pushed herself away from what appeared to be a man. She shuffled into something. Twisting to see, she found another man peering down at her, his expression unreadable. And next to him was a third.

"What do you want?" Emya said in a hoarse voice, her throat raw.

"You," the man before her said, his voice barely a whisper. "Safe."

This didn't mean much to Emya. She was a valuable magic source, but regardless she was at their mercy.

The man stood and held out his hand. Emya took it and he pulled her to her feet. Her legs felt like jelly. She took a few stumbling steps forward before toppling face-first into the dirt. She lay there for a while. By the sound of silence, she figured that the men had left. Yet, as she finally lifted her eyes, there they stood, motionless and watching her. Emya shakily got to her feet. The men offered no help. This time Emya managed to follow them without falling. She trudged with her eyes cast down, watching every step so that when they stopped, she didn't immediately see where they were.

"Emya!"

Her head jerked up. Felix engulfed her in what

felt like a bone-crushing hug. He wasn't holding her very tightly, yet her bones ached, and her skin burned. One of the men—they were much taller than Felix and Artyem, who were already very tall—placed a hand on Felix's shoulder and drew him away.

"Pain," he rasped. Felix gave him a long look before turning back to Emya.

"You're safe," Felix said, clasping his hands behind his back as if to stop himself from touching her. "I was sick with worry. Artyem is beside himself, between you being gone and me being unconscious. We lost the you know what for a while and he had to search the sands to find it."

Emya didn't know what to say, and she didn't have the energy to speak regardless. She let out a long sigh of relief and Felix seemed to understand.

"Come, just a bit further." He held his hand out and she took it, his fingers lightly gripped hers, stinging as they grasped. The looming villagers stepped out of their way as the two mages passed, their movements were smooth and silent, almost inhuman. Though they had saved her and let them move freely through the village, Emya couldn't shake the feeling of danger. Felix led her a short distance to a small hut. It was much nicer and well-built than the huts they had sheltered in at the abandoned village. A bright, crackling fire illuminated the small, clean room. The floor was paved with stone. There was furniture made from some of the strange wood with cushions of rough cloth and stuffed with feathers and wool from the feel. Felix helped her to a low couch, and she laid down on it gingerly.

"They have your sheep," he said, laying a blanket over her. She winced so badly that he quickly took it off.

"Sorry," he said anxiously. "I should have known better the moment I saw you in the light."

"What do you mean?" she asked.

He opened his mouth to answer then changed his mind, holding up a finger indicating that she should wait. He rummaged around the room a bit before returning with a piece of stone. He turned it over in his hand until it changed into a small, shiny mirror. Emya gasped. Her face was raw and angry red. On each cheek were large blisters.

"The Lim have some magic, though very limited, and their healing skills saved your life, but you are still gravely injured." He bit his lip worryingly.

"Can you heal me?" she asked tiredly, reclining onto the couch and closing her eyes.

"I'll do what I can, but injuries like yours, especially when they're inflicted by demons, take time to heal, even with magic."

"Time we don't have," she murmured.

"Sleep," he said. "Then you can tell me all about the new dire straits we're in."

"It's good news at least," she said. "Where is Artyem?"

"He's... consulting the village elders. He'll be back soon. They aren't talkers."

Emya hummed her understanding despite being close to sleep. The last thing she heard was the door opening.

~~*~*~*~*

"They seem to be aware of it," Artyem's quiet but aggravated words woke Emya. "And they do not want it here. They want us to leave."

"Are you sure you didn't misunderstand them?" Felix asked. "Are you sure they don't want us to leave and it to stay?"

"If they wanted to take it from us they could have done so already," Artyem said, his patience waning. "I know you don't trust them but use your head."

"They know I'm a powerful mage, that is certain. Maybe they don't want to fight me, but you saw how interested they were."

"Interest is not the same as want."

There was a long pause. Emya could imagine each of them attempting to influence the other with their stubbornness. She fully expected a fight, but to her surprise, Artyem sighed defeatedly.

"It is a moot point. We cannot move on until Emya is healed."

"I'm doing my best," Felix said. "She's stubborn you

know."

Artyem huffed a laugh. Emya pried her eyes open. The two men were sitting on the floor, backs against the couch she was sprawled out on.

"I'm feeling better," she said truthfully. Both their heads turned towards her sharply.

"You're doing better," Felix said with a grin. "Do you feel up to telling us your news?"

"I need some water," she said. Her mouth was so dry. Artyem produced a flask and helped her sit up. She then explained everything that had happened in as few words as possible. Felix's expression became darker and darker as she talked. Artyem was unreadable, but Emya knew by now that he was upset too.

"That makes a lot more sense," Felix said when she finished. "I always had a lot of questions about Azo and Fen. Couldn't ask them of course, but their behaviors and knowledge of magic just didn't add up for what I assumed about them."

"What are we going to do? We certainly can't leave the companion here for Azo to get," Emya said.

Felix frowned, scrunching his brow. "We can either bring it back and protect it in Civim or destroy it. Neither is a good option, but we've never had any good options."

"I say destroy it," Artyem said. "No one needs to know anything more about it."

"I agree, though it's easier said than done," Felix said. "That's a problem for later. We need to focus on getting to the fortress."

"Can we trust this Azo's directions? Might he simply try to kill us on the way and take the Companion?" Artyem asked.

"I doubt he will try to fight all three of us outright. He was always the more conniving of the pair. Fen was the brute force, but Azo will wait until after we've weakened ourselves trying to break the bond."

"I told him that we would fight him if you didn't agree to his deal," Emya said. "Maybe I shouldn't have given him the heads up."

Felix beamed at her. "You told him that?"

Emya nodded sheepishly.

"Well done! We want him to have his guard up. He doesn't think straight when he's stressed."

Emya smiled but inwardly she still worried. Even when Azo was not thinking straight, he was still very dangerous. She lay back while Artyem and Felix discussed plans to continue their journey. Felix thought one more full day and night would be enough time to heal Emya sufficiently. She slept through most of the day only waking occasionally to a tickling sensation and Felix kneeling over her, concentrating on his magic.

The next morning, Emya was feeling much better. She sat up and ate a strange porridge that the villagers had brought them. It looked like a bowl of pulverized stone, but it tasted sweet and smooth. The angry red blisters on her face had cleared up, though her skin was darker now, as though she had been out in the sun for a while. Felix was pacing the small room, impatient and ready to be moving on.

"You're going to wear a hole in the floor," Artyem said. He was sitting on the couch next to Emya, methodically cleaning his blades.

"In this old floor? I just might," he said, stopping. He sat on a little wooden chair across from Emya.

"Who are these people?" Emya asked, curious for the first time. She hadn't seen any of them since they had rescued her.

"We're not sure," Felix said. "They didn't speak our language at all when they found us, but they seemed to have picked up on a few words rather quickly. The raw magic doesn't affect their ability to reason, though they have some... quirks that are unsettling. The way they stare at each other for hours on end suggests they can hear each other's thoughts. They also hunt and eat the magical creatures here."

"Sometimes they cook them, sometimes they don't," Artyem added.

"Yes, but those creatures are so saturated in raw magic that no one should ever eat them, or go near them," Felix said distastefully.

"Felix said you went to talk to them the day I came here," Emya said to Artyem. "What were you talking about?"

"Very little," Artyem said. "I was attempting to

ascertain what exactly had happened to you, so Felix could better heal you."

"They weren't very helpful," Felix said.

They were interrupted by a gentle knock at the door. It opened and a small, hunched-over old woman shuffled in. In one hand she held a bundle of cloth made from sheep's wool. In the other were three small flasks. Silently Felix took the gifts and then the women indicated for him to give her the empty bowls.

After she left, Felix handed them each a flask and what appeared to be a cloak. Then he opened his flask and smelled it. His face wrinkled in disgust.

"What is it?" Emya asked.

"I'm not sure, but it smells awful."

"Should we pour it out once we are well away from the village?"

"No, I have a feeling this might be medicine, so we'll hold onto it."

Felix performed his cleaning-up magic on all of them so they could start the rest of their journey feeling as good as possible. Which she appreciated because as Emya stood, she realized she was not entirely back to normal. The world spun for a moment and her feet stung as if with a thousand needles. When it subsided, she was left with a dull ache in her feet and legs. Felix placed her cloak over her shoulders and secured it with a stone-like clasp in the front.

"How are you feeling?" he asked, though he already

knew, she was sure.

"I'm alright," she said. "I'm ready for this to be over."

"As am I," Artyem said.

Gathering their packs, they left the little house. Outside it was dim and dreary. Purple clouds covered the sky, though it wasn't raining... yet. In the light, the villagers were a slightly lighter gray, though still striking in appearance. Those who went about their day stopped when the trio passed and stood completely still. They looked like statues. It was indeed unsettling.

Little sheep wandered lazily through the village, munching on little tufts of vegetation. They were much woolier than the sheep in Emya's village. Their curly coats were almost spherical. Several of the sheep slowly pursued the trio as they strode through the village and then finally emerged onto the desert. A small group of older-looking villagers stood waiting, still as stone, watching Emya, Felix, and Artyem approach.

"Thank you for your hospitality," Felix said with a thin, uncomfortable smile. The elders nodded but said nothing. Felix looked over his shoulder at Emya and Artyem, shrugging one shoulder. He led them out into the desert. It was a very strange goodbye Emya thought, but then, she wouldn't have expected anything else.

No one spoke until they were a considerable distance away from the village. Then Artyem broke the silence.

"So, how are we to find this barrier? Did Azo give

you instructions?" he asked.

"No," Emya said. "He just said I will be able to find it because I am a descendant of Pike."

"We might just walk into it," Felix suggested.

"No," Emya said again. "Azo said we would just pass through it entirely and come out the other side."

"That's incredibly powerful magic," Felix said skeptically. "I'm not sure it's possible, even for the sorcerers of old."

"Well then maybe Azo is wrong. It wouldn't be the first time."

The trek through the desert was filled with the monsters and shadows of the realm, but Emya found she was able to fight them off better than before. The fire she summoned was stronger and she was able to aim at and direct it toward the creatures. Her shields were sturdier, and she could hold them up for longer periods. Felix said it was from all the practice she was getting, but Emya felt it was from something else. Ever since she had confronted Azo days before and had won their battle of wills, she felt more confident and powerful than she had ever felt before. No one would bully or frighten her into compliance ever again.

Given her newfound prowess, Felix started teaching her some fighting magic when they had a reprise from the creatures.

"It's not about being angry or scared," he said. "Those can fuel your magic, of course, but you must know how to disrupt the order of the world. Everything has order and patterns and structure. Some powerful enough forces will destroy that order. A lightning strike for example."

"A blade," Artyem added.

Emya nodded. "It's the opposite of constructive magic."

"Right," Felix said. "Kind of. In a way, it's a combination of constructive and elemental because the force you are creating must take the form of something. We use electricity, which is what lightning is because it is such a powerful element. The stronger and more practiced you become, the more powerful it will be."

"But we can use other elements too," Emya said. "Like fire."

"Yes. Water, air, even dirt, and minerals. If you know how you can disrupt the order and are skilled enough to direct the element, you can use just about anything."

"As with my blades," Artyem added. "I aim for weak points."

"Exactly," Felix said, nodding. "Yet, with magic, the better we understand the element and the substance we are trying to destroy; we can be much more precise."

"All weapons follow that same reasoning, non-magic weapons improve more slowly."

"Yes, you're right," Felix said. "Although, as our understanding of elemental magic increases, it has been used to create better non-magic weapons."

"What does element mean?" Emya asked. She hadn't learned much about that kind of magic despite hearing the word a lot.

"It means, in terms of magic, the most basic formation that can be manipulated by magic," Felix said. "Water, for example, is a magical element, but there is more to water than just water. Water in the ocean has salt. You can use magic to separate the water from the salt, but when you manipulate salt water, the salt is just along for the ride."

"Is salt not an element then?"

"We consider it to be one. We learn more every day about the world around us and how magic plays a role. The definition of what is an element has changed as we've made discoveries. It's so interesting. That's why I want to make it my field of study if the Masters let me."

Emya began to practice summoning the energy, electricity as Felix had called it and directing it at a new breed of ugly little monsters. These were more spheres than a creature and they used their shape to roll across the plains towards their prey. When Emya struck one with a blast of energy, it shot off into the air like it had been kicked. It was surprisingly entertaining. Pretty soon they were all laughing, even Artyem. Emya lost herself in the game they created and almost forgot where they were. As the day wore on, and their energy depleted, they returned to attacking the creatures only when they came too close. While they walked, they ate the strange food the villagers had given to them, and before long the sun was setting. All that was before them was a long stretch of desert.

As the sun began to sink below the horizon, Emya began to panic. Had Azo lied to her? Or were they just going the wrong way? Her steps slowed and she was just about to suggest they stop and consider their options when suddenly she was no longer in the desert.

~~*~*~*~*

Emya stumbled back and was in the desert once again. It had happened so fast she wasn't sure what she had seen. Artyem and Felix looked back at her with concern

"What's wrong," Felix asked. "You look frightened."

"Where did I go?" she asked breathlessly. "I was just in a..."

That seemed to add to his concern. "What?"

"A forest."

He and Artyem exchanged confused looks.

"Do you think it could have been a vision?" Artyem asked gently.

"I don't know, it felt—" Emya took a step towards her two companions and the forest appeared around her once more. "—Real."

She stepped back this time Felix and Artyem gasped in surprise, their distressed expression relaxing

147

with relief.

"Not a vision," Felix said. "You found the barrier."

"So how can we pass through it?" Artyem asked.

"Hmm." Felix's brow scrunched as he thought. "Let's try the simple solution first."

He took Emya by the hand and as she stepped forward, Felix was brought into the forest with her. Felix grinned. "I really didn't think that would work."

"What did you think would happen?"

"I don't know, maybe nothing, maybe something."

"Maybe it would kill you," Emya said flatly.

"Maybe," Felix shrugged.

"Well, it was easier to find than we thought," she said. "Do you think that's a bad sign? As though Messam wasn't too worried about anyone getting through because of what lurks within?"

"I doubt he would go to the trouble of creating the most powerful barrier known to mages if he thought there would be hordes of his descendants bringing all their friends through."

Emya shot him another incredulous look, he grinned unrepentantly.

"Enough, we have to go back for Artyem," Emya said. They turned and stepped back through the barrier, emerging to find Artyem looking stressed. When he saw them he relaxed.

"That worked then?" he asked.

"Yep," Felix said.

"And Emya can pass through it without any consequences?"

"As far as I know, and it didn't hurt me either. Thanks for asking."

Artyem shrugged. "Then it won't harm me."

Emya took Artyem's hand, she hadn't let go of Felix's, and they stepped into the forest. Other than the mass of overgrowth it looked entirely normal as if they had stepped out of the Twisted realm. It was mercifully cooler. Emya had grown used to the oppressive heat, but now the cool, light breeze uplifted her spirit. It carried scents of pine, freshly churned soil, and vegetation.

"This is an old forest," Felix said in a low voice. "Trees like this don't exist anymore."

"Pine trees?" Emya asked, who was sure she had seen several pine trees in the Tritium Mountains.

"They smell like pine but look at them, they're not."

Emya looked carefully at a nearby tree. It was very tall, and the trunk was gnarled with twisted and knotting bark. Its leaves were like pine needles but thicker and wound into spirals. They were very pretty.

"The fortress is in the center of these woods I presume," Artyem said.

"I think so," Emya said.

"So we need only go straight," Felix said. "But there's no telling how far it is."

Artyem and Felix began the arduous task of hacking a path through the growth. Emya was already worn

149

out from the journey and she worried her companions would be completely exhausted by the time they reached the fortress. She imagined wistfully of Felix magically transporting them back to Civim the moment they were free of the Companion. Of course, that would be impossible, but she could dream. Once they made it to the fortress, the journey was still far from over. On the other hand, if Azo was there and he decided to try to kill them rather than wait and see if they were able to free themselves from the Companion…

She shook her head slightly, determined not to worry about Azo. One crisis at a time. The forest became denser as they went. What little light pierced the canopy faded and Emya had to summon a flame for them to see by. The two men were sweating and panting despite the cool air, from the effort to clear the way. Emya stood by while they cleared a particularly dense and thorny patch of brush when out of the corner of her eye she saw a shimmering movement.

"Felix," she whispered as she spun on the spot, holding her flame aloft.

Felix straightened up and looked around. "What is it?"

"I don't know," Emya said baffled. "I saw something that looked… magic."

"You're going to have to be more specific," Felix said with a note of humor in his tone.

"It shimmered, like oil in water," she said.

Felix grimaced. "Oh, that kind of magic."

"What is it?"

"I don't know, but we're about to find out." He pointed behind her. Emya whirled around to find a mass of oily shimmer in the air. Something began to materialize. Someone grabbed her shoulder and pulled her back. Artyem and Felix stepped in front of her.

"Get ready to use fire," Felix said. "But if it doesn't work, you must make the strongest shield you can."

A piercing, gurgling cry emitted from the thing forming before them. Emya was surprised to find that she could understand the emotion behind it. Not anger, or fear, but pure glee. It was happy it found them, and even happier to kill them. The shimmering mass solidified into a creature of light. Tall and lanky its features were distinctive. It had a long head like a horse with lots of sharp, protruding bones beneath its bright flesh. Its long arms had three joints that spun like balls in sockets. It had too many fingers to count all ending in long, serrated blade-like claws. Its long legs bent inward at the knee, ending in the same deadly claws as its arms.

It attacked Artyem first, its claws connecting with his blades with a blow so strong it knocked Aryem on his back. Lightning burst from Felix's hands, enveloping the creature. It cried out in pain and anger, lashing out and knocking Felix away. It advanced on Emya. Summoning fire with as much power as she could and blasted the creature. The vegetation around it cooked, but it didn't react to the fire. It struck out with its claws just as Emya summoned a shield, but it still sent her flying. Her head smacked against a tree trunk. Stars burst into her vision. As they cleared, she saw Artyem was up once more, this time he was fighting the creature with a ferocity Emya had never seen. Each time it struck him with its claws the blow slipped off the blade and Artyem ducked and danced around the creature. Then Felix rose from the brush and joined the fray. He struck the creature with a blade, black as night. A blade made of magic, Emya realized. The trio danced, with the two men striking blow after blow as the creature cried out in pain. Finally, as it began to slow, wounded and weary, Felix struck its head, his blade sinking deep into the skull. The creature fell, shimmering, and faded away.

As it disappeared, Felix and Artyem sat on the ground panting. Emya climbed out of the brush and crawled over to them.

"Are you hurt?" she asked.

"Not badly," Artyem said, Felix nodded, trying to catch his breath.

"What was that?" Emya asked once Felix was able to speak again.

"No idea," he said, "But the magic is that of a guardian. A type of war magic used to create guards for the mages and their strongholds."

"Is that the only one?" Artyem asked.

"Not likely," Felix said, getting to his feet. "But we

must be close, and once we pass a certain point, they won't pursue us any longer, lest they damage the other protective magic of the fortress."

"Then we must be quick," Artyem said jumping to his feet and pulling Emya to hers.

The battle had cleared away the brush around them, saving them a little effort. It was still smoldering as they passed through. Luckily the foliage began to thin and soon they emerged onto a small field of overgrown grass. Rising before them was indeed a fortress. Its dark walls were smooth enough to reflect the moonlight above.

There was no visible door, and Felix concluded they had to walk along the wall until they found one. The forest had grown close to the walls and was difficult to cut through. After about an hour they found themselves back at the clearing.

"It seems there is no way in," Artyem said. "Perhaps this is another barrier only Emya can pass through?"

Emya ran her hand along the part of the wall that was exposed to the clearing. It was just large enough for a portcullis to be, though none appeared, nor did she pass through as she had the barrier.

"It must be here though," Emya said. "Why else would this be the only place not completely overgrown?"

"The passage might be hidden under a spell," Felix said, examining the wall. "It's impossible to guess what kind of magic was used, but it might be possible to force the magic to reveal itself. Then it might be broken by force."

Artyem shrugged and began flattening some of the tall grass. When he was done, he set his cloak down and he and Emya sat while Felix stood with his hand on the wall, eyes closed, and head bowed in concentration.

"There is something," Felix said after some time, "concealed by magic."

Artyem and Emya pulled out some of the hard, gray cheese and a dense bread that was filled with something with the texture of dried fruit but was quite savory. It also had something crunchy, almost like nuts, but not quite.

"I know we've been eating this but is it safe?" she asked Artyem.

"It hasn't made us sick," Artyem said. "Best not to think past that."

Emya nodded. It was well into the night before Felix spoke again. Emya was dozing on Artyem's shoulder when his triumphant voice cut through.

"I've got it!"

"You found the door?" she mumbled, blinking rapidly to clear her vision.

"No," he said and her heart sank. She was eager to be finished and every obstacle was maddening. "I've figured out the magic that was used. It's not a blood enchantment, thankfully, but it's not going to be easy to break."

"You can break it though?" she asked.

"All enchantments can be broken," Felix said, running his hands along the wall until he settled on a spot just off-center. "The problem is what else breaks in the process."

"Could it hurt us?" Emya asked, worried.

"Oh yes," Felix said. "It could harm us both physically and mentally, like what happened to your village."

"How do you break it?" Artyem asked.

"Emya and I will channel our power into it until it shatters. Nothing elegant."

"Which is why it's not safe," Artyem stated. "Like glass flying everywhere."

"Yeah, kind of," Felix said.

"What happens if we break it but are too worn out to fight whatever is in the fortress?" Emya asked.

"We'll just have to figure that out," Felix said grimly. "We're so close, but we're beyond most of my knowledge of this fortress and its master."

Felix showed Emya the magic. Emya pressed her hand against the wall, willing her magic to find the enchantment. For a while she felt nothing until suddenly it was there, pulsing gently against her magic. Once found it was hard to ignore. It had an energy that was strange and unsettling. It was like reaching through the dark in an empty room and touching something slimy.

"What do I do now?" she asked, unable to mask the revulsion in her voice. She had always directed magic into something she could picture, something she wanted. Now she could neither picture what she wanted to channel the magic into, nor did she want to.

"Force your magic into it like stuffing a bag so full it bursts. Give it a try."

Emya pressed her hand against the wall once more and did as Felix directed. It was easier than she expected. The enchantment sucked her magic away readily. She stopped quickly as it felt too much like the companion.

"I don't like that," she said.

"Me neither," he said. "Are you ready?"

Emya nodded, placing her hand back on the wall.

"Go!"

Emya let the enchantment take her magic. She trusted Felix, but as it sucked away more and more, she began to panic.

"It's working," Felix said just as she was about to wail in fear. And indeed, she realized, it wasn't taking her magic as quickly, and it felt... bloated. It began to push back, physically forcing her away. She put her whole weight against her hand. With the last fiber of her being, she blasted it with magic until she collapsed on the ground, Felix fell a few moments later.

"Did it work?" Artyem ran over and crouched next to them.

"Give it a moment," Felix said.

For a few minutes, nothing happened. Emya

couldn't feel the spell anymore. Then a wave of heat burst from the wall. The dark stone burst instantly into a purplish powder that dissolved into nothing before it touched the ground. Behind it was a gilded portcullis. Emya lay back on the ground, exhausted. If she fell asleep, she might not wake for days.

Felix groaned. "I feel how I used to feel when Azo and Fen drained me."

A pang of regret stung Emya. She didn't want to open wounds that hadn't healed much, if at all. But as Felix slowly got to his feet, he didn't appear to be upset. In fact, she was sure he wasn't.

"Maybe you both should rest," Artyem said, ever practical. "You will need your full strength for whatever lies within."

"I agree," Felix said. "But let's rest inside. We may be safe from the guardian but that doesn't mean something else won't come along."

"You don't know what's in there either."

"Fine, which do you prefer?"

Artyem considered for a moment, then said, "Inside."

The gilded portcullis lifted almost silently as they approached.

"Never a good sign in all the old stories," Artyem muttered. Felix shot him a grin.

"What stories?" Emya asked as they passed into a courtyard bathed in delicate moonlight. Emya hadn't known what to expect, but after the carefully crafted magic of Civim, the overgrown, crumbling courtyard seemed out of place. It was over a thousand years old, she supposed, but from what she had heard about the sorcerers, she had expected some kind of everlasting spell to have preserved the fortress.

"Old tales about the days of the sorcerers," Felix said. "Most are embellished for entertainment. Whenever the hero journeyed into a sorcerer's fortress, it would seem to welcome him in. Then the doors would close and lock and the hero would have to fight monsters and escape from traps."

"Do you think there are monsters in here?" Emya worried. She had hoped to feel as though the worst was over when they reached the fortress, but now she felt more afraid.

"Maybe, but I don't think many of the monsters we've come across are powerful enough to get in." Felix said. "But there are almost certainly traps."

Artyem gazed around the courtyard until he found a spot that he deemed safe enough for them to rest. Emya curled up next to Felix. Warmth and relief coursed through her and she didn't know if it was hers or Felix's, but she figured he felt the same as she did about having made it this far. Their journey was almost over, whatever the outcome. For a moment she wished they weren't going to be separated, but that feeling faded as she drifted into sleep.

They didn't sleep long. Soon the hard ground and her many aches and pains woke Emya. She carefully shifted Felix's arm off her shoulder, but he woke as well, and sat up, looking around blearily for Artyem, who was sitting on a fallen stone column nearby.

"How long did we sleep?" Felix mumbled tiredly.

"Near four hours," Artyem replied, his tone suggesting he didn't think that was nearly long enough.

"Good," Felix said, getting to his feet. Emya still felt drained and didn't think she would have much strength for magic. Her eyes met Artyem's in silent agreement.

Emya stood, brushed off her tunic, and looked around. It was still dark, but she could see more clearly and the fortress beyond the courtyard was intimidating. The stone she thought was black was actually a dark purple, and the main entrance was a set of huge iron doors covered in short spikes. Would it open for them as the portcullis had?

Felix took the lead, ignoring the imposing door and instead, leading them to a smaller servant door. Did a sorcerer need servants? Emya supposed Messam couldn't be bothered with mundane things like cooking or cleaning, even with magic. Inside, Felix conjured a small sphere of light and held it up to illuminate the bare walls.

"Where shall we look?" Emya asked.

"We need to find Messam's study, that's where he would conduct his magical experiments," Felix said, taking a few cautious steps forward.

"Unless he was as disorganized as you are," Artyem teased. "Then it could be anywhere."

Felix laughed, "Indeed."

His light blinked out. As if struck by an arrow, something cold pierced Emya's heart, freezing her to the spot. The paralyzing cold spread through her and whispered in her head. It wanted her dead. It was pure evil. Soon she could no longer draw breath.

Chapter Eight

Emya's chest burned with invisible fire. Her lungs screamed for air, yet she could not oblige. As her consciousness began to fade, she wondered bitterly why Pike Messam had allowed his descendants to find his fortress if he was just going to kill them the moment they walked in. All at once, she sucked in a breath, her heart began to pump again, and she stumbled forward, sucking in each beautiful breath hungrily.

"Felix?" she breathed. "Artyem?"

She did not hear them breathing, and feeling around in the dark, she only found one of them.

"They're my friends," she pleaded with the invisible force. "Release them."

Nothing happened. They were going to die soon.

She summoned her magic, trying to find the curse the same way Felix had found the magic that hid the door. She imagined the magic enclosing them, suffocating them. After a moment she did feel something-- energy. She sent a desperate bolt of power through whoever she was holding onto. There was a sudden, desperate intake of breath, and then coughing.

"Are you okay?" she asked in a high, teary voice.

"Yes." It was Felix, who she was holding onto.

Artyem was the one coughing, but he managed to speak through the fit. "Just barely."

"How did you get out of it, Emya?" Felix asked when he caught his breath.

"I don't know. I was just thinking about how stupid it was that I got in here because I was Messam's descendant, but his magic was going to kill me all the same. Then it let me go. It wouldn't let you two go though. I found the enchantment the way you did and broke it by force. It worked quite easily."

Felix let out a sound of awe. "well done, we were lucky then. It felt like an incredibly powerful enchantment. Likely meant to kill the kind of mage who could get through the barrier by force. There was nothing I could do."

"Indeed," Artyem said quietly. "But that was an old enchantment, just as everything in here is. Most magic grows weaker with age, but some can grow stronger, like petrified wood."

"Yes," Felix said. "We still must be careful."

It was decided that Artyem would lead the way, but Felix would look for enchantments, as he didn't need to be in front to detect them. Artyem's blades, Felix said, might be able to destroy weakened curses, especially with their magic-resistant properties.

"There have been blades forged to cut through magic," Artyem explained, "though none remain, and the art has been lost. They're the kind of weapon the sorcerers despised most."

"And so the sorcerers hunted and killed the sword makers, I suppose?" Emya said.

"Yes, brutally."

They left the servants' passage a little way down and entered a long room that reminded Emya of her village's council chamber. There was a large fireplace and several torch holders along the walls that lit up with bright fire when they entered. A long wooden table, covered in a shimmering blue tablecloth, was laid out for a meal, though there was no food set out.

"If this is the main dining chamber," Felix said, "then the study must be above. Since he needed such a large fireplace, the chimney would be combined."

"There's no direct way there from this room," Artyem said, looking around as he spoke. "Though maybe there's a servant's staircase somewhere nearby."

Emya didn't want to take another servant's way. Perhaps the mighty sorcerer, in all his wisdom, had laid traps in all the surreptitious routes since that was the way someone with bad intentions would most likely go.

Another servant's door at the other end of the hall entered the kitchen, which led back outside. Felix decided to lead them back through the dining hall and the more ornate doors into a large, dilapidated foyer with a grand staircase. It must have been magnificent, Emya thought, with all the ragged tapestries and threadbare rugs that were once very fine. They climbed the staircase, which creaked and wobbled. At the top was a dark, narrow hallway, though not as narrow as the servant's passage.

"Strange," Felix said. "One would expect some sort of reception room for the guests of honor to meet before descending the stairs."

"This isn't a palace for parties and court," Artyem said. "It's a war fortress."

"I know, but then why does it need a grand staircase and all that finery?"

"Perhaps it used to be a palace?" Emya suggested.

"Exactly," Felix said.

"Why does that matter?" Artyem asked irritably.

"Because it tells us something about the place," Felix said. "Messam converted a palace into a fortress, so he might not have been able to build a study above the dining room. The space would already have been taken up by many rooms. He might have converted a ballroom instead. But the reception room is missing, so he changed something up here."

They tread quietly down the hallway, Felix holding up a small ball of light to guide them. Though there were many door frames along the wall, all had been filled in. Whatever kind of sorcerer Pike Messam was, Emya thought, he did not care to use his magic to make the place look nice. The finery certainly hadn't come from him.

They rounded a corner and about halfway down the second corridor they found a set of iron double doors covered in long sharp spikes.

"Welcoming," Artyem said with his usual dry sarcasm. "Do you think this is the study?"

"It could be," Felix said. "But it doesn't seem right. Why would a sorcerer need to deter people with spikes? Magic would serve him much better."

"Do we go in?" Artyem asked.

"Might as well see what he's hiding," Felix said. With considerable effort, he and Artyem pulled the doors open. Emya peered into the pitch black. Felix held up his light and they wandered inside. The room was filled with devices of torture. Skeletal remains were piled in the middle of the room.

"Oh," Felix breathed.

"Sick," Artyem said. Emya was speechless. Never had she seen such awful-looking devices.

"Let's move on," Felix said practically. As he and Artyem were closing the door, there was a long, cold, piercing wail that froze them to the spot.

"What is that?" Emya whispered.

"I don't know," Felix said.

Artyem pushed through them and strode briskly down the hallway. "Let's get moving."

Emya and Felix followed quickly, but they had barely gone halfway down the hall before something seemed to materialize before them. It was not wholly there, as Emya could see through it to the other side of the hallway. The exit. It let out the same wail they had heard and flew towards them at an unearthly speed. Artyem cut through it as it passed through him and it screamed in agony. Still, it emerged whole and flew at Felix, and before Felix could conjure anything that might stop it, the thing flew into him. His eyes went wide, his back rigid. Emya was alarmed to see that he had stopped breathing.

"Felix," she gently shook his shoulder. "What's happening to him?"

"The spirit is attacking him from the inside," Artyem said, pulling Emya aside, his blade held aloft in the other hand. At first, Emya thought he was going to stab Felix, and she let out a yelp of terror. Then Artyem lowered the blade pressing the broad side against Felix's chest. He shook and convulsed frightfully, though Artyem held him tight, so he didn't fall over.

Mist burst from Felix, and he collapsed into Artyem's arms. The mist swirled about but couldn't seem to reconstitute. It slowly faded away until they were left in the dark empty hallway. The only sound was Felix's haggard breathing.

"That's despicable," Felix said when he caught his breath. "I knew some of the sorcerers practiced spirit magic, but I never dreamed of seeing it for myself."

"Spirt magic?" Emya muttered.

"Magic that tears the soul from the body. It's horrible, dark magic."

"Do you think there are more?" Artyem asked.

"Undoubtedly. Let's move quickly and try not to disturb any more spirits."

This proved easier said than done, as it seemed as if opening the iron door had let the spirits out. They materialized around every corner. Artyem's blades cut through and weakened them. Felix tried a few spells too, but nothing deterred them, not even fire. It was such a fight getting through the many halls and rooms that when they passed through a small door into a dark room, it was a surprise that the spirit following them suddenly stopped. It seemed that it could not pass the threshold. With a quick flick of his wrist, Artyem sliced through the spirit in the doorway. It burst into mist and dissipated.

"Whatever this room is, the sorcerer didn't want his abominations getting in," Artyem said, sheathing his blade.

"Perhaps it's the study?" Emya speculated.

Felix held up his light and walked around. The room was not very big. Decaying wooden shelves lined the walls. Set upon them were jars with strange contents. Some were filled with liquids that shimmered as the light passed.

"It's a storage room," Felix said as he passed a shelf of oddly shaped items. "Might be some of his failed experiments?"

Then a ripple of energy, Emya didn't know how else to describe it, passed through the room.

"We should go," Artyem said in a low, urgent tone. "Now."

Felix spun on his heels and marched towards the door, Emya and Artyem falling into step behind him. They turned and continued down the corridor until they came to a large window. The moon shined in, illuminating the dilapidated ornate rug that was the only ornament between the windows and the bare walls. As Felix stepped into the light Emya gasped, stopping short.

"Felix! Your skin!"

Felix looked down at his hands. Small flesh-colored drops fell onto the carpet.

"Don't come into the light," Felix warned Emya and Artyem, even as his skin dripped into his mouth. It didn't matter though, Emya found her flesh melting away in the darkness.

"A curse," Artyem said. Patches of red marred his

frightened features.

Emya looked pleadingly at Felix, though she knew he had no answer.

"We must hurry and find the study. There may be an answer there. It can't be far now."

Moving proved to be too difficult. Emya's feet burned against the ground. She fell to her knees and rolled onto her back, gasping for breath. Someone was beside her, though she no longer could see anything except for darkness.

"Felix," she called desperately. "Fe-"

She couldn't breathe, her lungs were full of liquid or had liquefied themselves. As darkness crept over her and she resigned herself to the end. Yet it didn't come. The pain in her chest faded, though it still felt full of liquid. She was still in the hall with the large windows and the moonlight shining in, but it was now filled with water. She looked around in amazement. Artem was behind her, his eyes still closed. Felix was before her, a soft shroud of light wrapped around him. The light quickly spread out, filling the room and blinding Emya. Then it was gone along with the water. Emya hit the floor hard, bumping her head on Artyem's knee. When she managed to gather her wits, she noticed she was completely dry.

A dark figure loomed over her. It reached down and pulled her into a seated position.

"Are you alright?" The figure was Felix.

"I don't know," Emya said, still in a daze.

"What happened?" Artyem asked softly, sounding just as confused as Emya.

"I'm not sure," Felix said. "I was trying a form of counter magic. Washing a curse away with pure water, and then I think the Companion stepped in when it seemed as though we were going to die. But it saved you too, Artyem, so I don't know what exactly happened."

"Maybe the curse could only be broken for all of us at once?" Artyem suggested, getting to his feet. Emya was getting used to the low light again and peered at each man in turn. They didn't seem to be injured.

"That's not how curses usually work," Felix said. "But who knows."

Satisfied that Felix and Artyem were okay, Emya checked herself. Except for the throbbing part of her head that had struck Artyem, she felt alright. Though she hadn't sensed the Companion when it saved them, she wasn't surprised. It wasn't keen on their deaths unless they were trying to abandon it.

"Why didn't it save us from the first enchantment?" Emya asked. "We were going to die then too."

"I have no idea," Felix said. "Who knows what it's capable of?"

Artyem straightened his tunic, picked his blades up from where they had fallen, and secured them in their sheaths. Then he turned to Felix, his posture authoritative and determined.

"This fortress is too big. We must split up. You go alone. You'll go much faster as you have a better idea of what we're looking for. Emya and I will search the rest of this level." Artyem pulled a message stone out of a pocket, and one of his blades from its sheath.

"Alright." Felix took the stone and blade reluctantly. "We check in at every room we enter. If I don't hear from you for more than ten minutes, I'm coming to find you."

At first, Emya keenly felt the fear of being separated from Felix—his as well as her own—and she stayed close to Artyem. Though they came across spirits, many of them didn't seem to notice the pair, and the few that attacked seemed to do so half-heartedly.

"Perhaps they've grown tired of us?" Artyem suggested as they stepped into a small sitting room. He quickly pressed the stone between his thumb and forefinger.

"Maybe they're tired of getting slashed by your blades," Emya said, looking around the room for any books or papers. Finding none, she and Artyem continued to the next room.

"How long do you think this will take?" Emya asked as they entered another room, this one bare except for a large table and a few moth-eaten maps spread out on it. Emya didn't recognize any of the places on the maps, though she still knew very little about geography.

"To search this whole fortress, without finding anything to free you, could take days, even weeks,"

Artyem said, pulling out the stone. "Though I think we will find the study before the sun rises."

"Felix found some more trouble," he added, looking at the stone. "Another curse, though not as deadly as the last one. He was able to destroy it easily."

Emya didn't want to think about what might happen if she and Artyem encountered another curse.

"Do you think we'll be able to break the bond of the Companion?" she asked instead. Artyem stopped short of entering another room and peered at her contemplatively.

"I don't know," he said slowly. "Even if there is a way, there is no guarantee even Felix could wield it. Powerful though he is."

"He can wield the Companion," she said.

"Yes, but the magic to break the bond might be stronger, or more complex. Whatever the outcome, you needn't worry. Felix will find a way for you and him to live with it, and I will protect you both."

Artyem suddenly pulled out the stone and peered at it.

"Felix has found it," he said. "He's coming to meet us."

As they left the room they were in, Felix came running down the hall towards them looking very pleased with himself.

"This way!" he called, not waiting for them to catch up with him before taking off in the direction he had come. He led them upstairs and around three corners before he stopped at a set of unassuming double doors. Inside was not as Emya expected. There was nothing but a small round table in the middle of a room illuminated by a wall of windows. On it was a small box no bigger than Emya's fist.

"Felix," Emya said nervously. "This is the study?"

Artyem gave Felix a confused look.

"It's in the box," Felix said. "Exactly what we need."

Emya stepped up to the table and examined the plain, wooden box. It was lacquered in black and, though she didn't understand why, it gave her a sense of unease. This was unlike Felix's emotions, as he was quite relaxed, almost bored. She turned and looked back at Felix. He had a triumphant grin on his face. He motioned excitedly for her to open the box.

"That's... Not Felix," Emya said. Artyem turned to look at Felix, brow furrowed.

Felix's image laughed. "What do you mean? Of course, I am."

"No," Emya said. "I can feel Felix's emotion. He's not excited, he's bored."

Felix just smiled at her. "What do you mean, Emya? Of course, I'm excited."

Swoosh! Artyem's blade cut through Felix's form. There was no spray of blood as Felix's smiling doppelganger rippled and continued smiling. Emya, filled with rage at being tricked once again, summoned fire and blasted it at the image. Still, the thing was unmoved. It advanced on Emya, grin affixed.

"Open the box, Emya," it said. "It's everything you want. Everything you need."

Emya backed up into the table.

"Pick it up. Open it," the thing insisted.

"Emya! Move!"

Emya leaped to her right, landing on the floor in a heap. She turned to see Artyem bring his blade down in a sweeping arc to stab the box. The image of Felix screamed and disappeared. Sheathing the blade, Artyem held out a hand to Emya and pulled her to her feet.

"At least that was an easy trap," Artyem said. "It could have been much worse."

"What do you think was in the box?"

Artyem gave her a very serious look. "Everything we could ever want."

Emya stiffened with sudden unease, then Artyem smiled. "Just kidding. I have no idea. Probably another curse."

"You've been cursed again?"

Emya and Artyem turned to see Felix stepping into the room. Artyem gave Emya a questioning look. Emya could feel Felix's sudden confusion.

"He's the real Felix," Emya assured Artyem.

"Real?" Felix said, confused. Artyem explained what had happened.

"It's a very good thing you didn't open that box," Felix said. "It was indeed a curse."

"I suppose you didn't find the study after all?" Emya said.

"No," Felix said. "I felt your distress, so I came to find you, but as I was on my way, I think I found a secret passage. Let's all go together."

"You think it will be dangerous?" Emya asked.

"Undoubtedly, but it's where I would hide a study."

Artyem strode towards the door. "Let's go before we get into any more trouble."

"Let's go and get into more trouble you mean?" Felix said with a laugh.

"Yeah."

Though Felix seemed relieved and glad to see they were okay, Emya could feel his apprehension and tension. The passage was very well concealed. Felix had knocked over a table in his rush to get to them. The table had scraped the wall, which appeared to be solid stone except where the stone was torn like paper. Emya had never seen such a detailed rendering. She examined the paper as Felix and Artyem pulled it away. It was not painted but etched and inked.

"Here we go," Felix said after examining what they had uncovered. It was a small, narrow door with no handle, but it creaked open when Felix pushed it. He held up his light. Before them was a narrow, winding staircase.

"Won't be easy for me to use my knives in there," Artyem said. "I shall go first, so I have as much room as possible."

He squeezed through the passage. Felix indicated that Emya should follow him. Being the smallest, it was easy for her to slip through, but her shoulders barely cleared the passage walls. Felix and Artyem had to walk slightly sideways.

"How did the sorcerer get through here?" Emya asked.

"They were a lot smaller back then," Felix said in a hushed voice. "That, or Messam liked making it difficult for himself to get around."

As they descended the many steps, the walls began to shrink until they could go no further.

"This is a tunnel to nowhere Felix," Artyem said when he could no longer fit through the passage.

"Is there a wall?" Felix asked. Neither he nor Emya could see past Artyem.

"No, it keeps going, but no one can fit through to the end."

"Then it goes somewhere," Felix said. "We either need to make the passage bigger or ourselves smaller."

"The passage," Artyem said firmly.

"This should be a fun bit of magic," Felix said pushing past Emya and then Artyem. "Especially since I don't know what I'll be expanding into."

Felix placed his hands on the ceiling and pushed

the passage up. He did the same with each wall. The stairs they were on stayed the same size, creating a gap between them and the wall.

"Not too bad," Felix said. "Seems he designed it to expand. That's good. I was worried we might be near the sewer by now."

They descended the short way to the bottom of the passage where a small door was nestled between two large, ugly statues of some creature Emya had never seen before.

"What are those?" she gestured to the statues.

"Gargoyles," Felix said. "A mythical creature."

"Still," Artyem said. "The statues might be enchanted."

"I don't think so," Felix said, running his hand over the stone. "They're made of magic repressing stone. We're in the right place. These are meant to protect the outside from whatever is within."

Felix tried the door. It was not locked and he pushed it in without trouble. As he walked in and held up the light in his hand tiny sparks flew from it and suddenly the whole room was lit by dim, bluish sconces. It was exactly the kind of place Emya would expect a sorcerer to create dangerous magical devices. Shelves lined the walls, housing books and scrolls, bottles filled with strange liquid, materials like stone and metal, and half-finished creations that rose at least three stories to a ceiling of glass. The moon was just visible overhead.

"If there is something that can free us," Felix said, "it must be in here."

~~*~*~*~*

They searched the chamber but found nothing of interest. The shelves were stacked with books, non-magical odds and ends, and some enchanted items that Felix examined and determined were nothing more than simple magical devices for things like sending messages or watering a potted plant. All the books within the chamber were written in the ancient language. Emya looked around the room for a while before settling at the long table in the center of the room next to Felix, who sat at the head with Artyem on his other side. After a while, Artyem began to clean his blades. Emya, curious and bored, began to question Felix about what he was reading.

"I don't know," Felix said with barely concealed annoyance. "The dialect is archaic and hard to understand. Please be quiet, I need to think."

Exasperated by Felix, which he felt as well as her, she stood and walked around the room. It wasn't just the incomprehensible books that were bothering him, Emya felt on edge. Something about the room irritated her. As she paced around the room, she noticed that one part of the room aggravated her more than anything. Every time she came to it, she moved more swiftly past.

Stopping a few feet away from the spot the moment she realized this, she backtracked until she was overwhelmed by a sense of disgust. Her insides squirmed with the desire to turn and walk away. Resisting the urge, Emya peered at a small corner shelf. Most of the items were innocuous but pushed back in the dark was something that gazing upon sent tremors through her whole body. It appeared to be a half-finished stone carving. She wanted to smash it on the ground. Or something inside her did.

With immense self-control, she picked it up and turned it over in her hands. She couldn't imagine what the artist had in mind. Maybe a cloud or a pile of soap bubbles? Beneath it was a crumpled piece of parchment. Emya took it out. On it was a script in the ancient language. She brought her discovery over to the table.

Felix looked up at her as she approached, an expression of disgust and pure hatred overcame him.

"Put that down," he spat vehemently. Emya stopped short.

"Why?" she asked. She felt his anger, but she didn't understand it any more than she understood her own. "What is it?"

"Because it's bad. It's putrid and horrible. Probably cursed. Let's destroy it now before we find out."

Emya glanced at Artyem, who was looking between them in confusion.

"Why did you pick it up Emya?" Artyem asked. "It could be dangerous."

Emya looked down at the thing. It didn't look revolting, yet she wanted to throw it across the room. Something inside her despised the little carving, but that something wasn't her. Instead of doing as Felix said, she held out the piece of paper to him.

"At least look at this before we go smashing things," she said, ever practical, and handed him the parchment. At least he wasn't disgusted by that. As he read through it, his expression changed to astonishment.

"I think this is it," he murmured.

"The thing that will break the companion's bond?" Artyem asked excitedly.

"Not just that," Felix said breathlessly. "This could break any kind of bond or connection, magical or otherwise."

"Great," said Artyem. "How does it work?"

"It doesn't," Felix said flatly. "It was never finished."

Artyem hung his head. "So, we must keep looking."

Emya's heart sank. She hadn't even noticed how light it had become.

"Not necessarily," Felix said. "I might be able to finish it, at least enough so that it can break the Companion's bond."

Artyem huffed in frustration and then walked across the room to the windows. Then turned back to Felix.

"You've never done magic like this," he said. "What makes you think you can fix it?"

"I've studied magic like this. Just because we don't make dangerous magical weapons doesn't mean we can't"

Artyem held up a hand, his features becoming hard. Emya interrupted. "Magic is different now."

"What?" Felix asked, surprised.

"Azo told me. Magic isn't the same as it was when Messam was alive."

Felix looked at the object in his hand contemplatively.

"That's true," he said. "Which is perhaps the real reason I want to try to finish it. Imagine what I might learn."

"Your curiosity will be the death of you someday," Artyem said. "Let us hope it is not this day."

"Agreed, but if I am successful, I will save myself and Emya. So, this at least is a worthy gamble."

While Emya and Artyem made themselves comfortable on the threadbare rug with a bed of their cloaks. Felix sat down at the long table and set to work. Artyem took out the last of their food and split it into three portions. He handed Emya the gray food which she ate without tasting, glancing over at Felix every few minutes. He worked with his head bent close to the table, occasional sparks of light bursting from either the object or his fingers, she couldn't always tell.

After she finished eating, Emya wrapped her cloak around her, pillowed her head on her pack, and drifted off. When her eyes flickered open, sunlight was streaming through the ceiling. Felix worked all through the day. He didn't say much, and Artyem had to insist he eat the food they had set aside for him. Emya was beginning to think he might give up as the sound of frustrated noises and mumbled curses increased as the day grew late. Then, as Emya was contemplating opening a jar of strange, glittery black liquid, Felix's voice snapped her back to reality.

"I think I did it!" he said. Emya turned and hurried over to the table. Artyem strode over from the window.

"It can break the Companion's hold on us?" Emya asked excitedly.

"I think so," Felix said. Artyem was silent, but a glance at his furrowed brow and lips pressed into a thin line told Emya he was afraid for them.

"How does it work?" Emya asked. Apprehension and excitement fought for her attention.

Felix picked up his pack and set it on the table. He reached in and pulled out the Companion. Emya hadn't seen it since before they entered the Twisted Realm. It had become an iridescent silver, like moonlight reflecting off a still lake. She felt it now, its grip cold and tight on her magic.

"Well, that's the catch. For it to break the bond, we have to use the Companion's magic. You're going to have to use it to take my magic."

Horrified, Emya shook her head. Images flashed through her mind. Felix on the floor as his magic flowed out from him while the Kings drew symbols in it. Except in their place was Emya. "I can't do that! Not to you. I won't."

"You must," Felix insisted. "It's the only way."

"Emya," Artyem said quietly. "This is your best chance."

Emya turned to look at him. Though he'd been against everything from the start and concerned for their safety, now he wanted her to hurt Felix, maybe even kill him.

"You won't hurt me," Felix insisted. "I've done this to you, remember? You just have to take a little."

"Does she know how?" Artyem asked.

"Of course, all she has to do is ask."

Emya had never considered talking to the Companion, let alone asking it anything. She was always too repulsed by it to wonder how to use it. Felix took the Companion in his hands and held it out to her. Reluctantly she took it.

"In your mind, ask it to take my magic," Felix said. "It will obey you through your connection to it."

Her heart pounding, she gave Felix one more pleading look then turned her gaze back down to the Companion. It grew warm in her hands, almost as if it was excited about what she was going to do. When she closed her eyes, she could see the connection in her mind. She opened her eyes and found a cord of white light between her, the Companion, and Felix. The cord of light twisted and looped around her, wrapping tightly around her arms, legs, and torso converging into a thick rope in her middle where she drew her magic from. Felix, on the other hand, was not tangled in the cords of light. Instead, the cord split into five tightly wound, spiraling loops that connected to points in his chest around his heart. With the barest desire, little more than an inkling, power surged through her as a river and Felix collapsed in a heap.

Chapter Nine

"I'm fine," Felix said, lifting his head with effort. "Artyem, give it to me!"

In two long strides, Artyem grabbed the object and placed it in Felix's shaking hands. Emya couldn't control how much power she was taking, try as she might. Power flowed into her.

Felix couldn't hold his head up, but his lips moved silently and there was a bright, yellow, searing light that burned like fire. Emya stumbled and fell, her head hitting the floor hard. When she opened her eyes, it took a few moments for her vision to clear. Felix was on the ground, Artyem kneeling next to him. Emya could barely sit up. With a tremendous effort, she got to her hands and knees and crawled over to Felix. He was on his back, his head lolling next to his shoulder. To her horror, a long thin cord of magic still stretched from him to the Companion that had rolled across the room, though it faded from view.

"It didn't work," she cried in frustration.

"How can you tell?" Artyem asked.

"I can see the connection," she said, then looked down at herself. The cord that had connected her was gone. "No, it's only connected to Felix. I've been released."

She had been attached to the Companion for so long that she hadn't realized how much it had been holding her back. She felt like she could do anything with her magic. Summoning it with ease, she placed her hand against Felix's forehead. She had never healed anyone before, but all she wanted was for Felix to wake up. With a gentle prod of her magic, he did.

"Did it work?" he asked, slowly bringing his hand up to his eyes and rubbing them.

"It released Emya," Artyem said. Felix let his hand fall by his side with a sigh.

"She's safe then," he said.

"Yes, but it did not break your bond," Artyem explained.

Felix nodded. "I tried to break it for both of us, but I found that if I broke mine too that I would likely die. It is so tightly bound to my magic, the only way to break it would be to drain my magic until it's nearly dry. If I gave

186

Emya that much power, I wasn't sure I would be able to break her bond."

"Then what are we to do? Bring it back with you still attached?" Artyem asked.

"No," Felix said. "Take Emya home. I'll stay here and try to free myself."

"We're not leaving you," Emya said sternly. "I won't go."

Felix sighed and put his hands on his head.

"Are you sure if you lose enough of your magic you will be able to break it?" Artyem asked quietly. "How do you know?"

"Like most things, I don't know, but that's what I saw. Emya was twisted up in a bright cord of light, and if I broke her bond, I could see that the Companion's hold would unravel, like cutting knotted twine. But mine..." He paused, at a loss for what to say.

"It was as if one good tug would pull your heart from your chest," Emya said, for that was what she had felt. Even as she sucked the magic from him she could feel the strain on the spiraled cords.

"Yes, I always felt pain in my chest when the Kings would drain me."

Artyem's brow furrowed in confusion. "I don't understand, surely cutting the cord would not harm you?"

"The cords are our own magic, manipulated by the Companion, the longer we are connected, the stronger its hold becomes. That much I'm sure. However, and I'm just guessing but I have long suspected the Companion uses the mage's skill and control of magic to further strengthen the bond. I think Emya is tangled in the cords because her control over her magic is not well developed and the Companion cannot develop it for her. As she increases her skill and untangles the web, the Companion winds the magic into a tighter grip."

Artyem looked at him with a mixture of frustration and indignation. "How long have you known this?"

"I suspected it with the Kings but it wasn't until our experiments in Civim that I saw the cords that bound Emya and began to refine my theory."

"And yet you still allowed her to learn magic?"

"Yes," Felix said defiantly. "Because all of this is just a theory. I don't know what the companion might do to her if she didn't refine her skill. I'm doing the best I can Tyem. I Swear."

Artyem gave Felix a long, hard look, then the fight drained from him with a long sigh.

"Then give it to me," he said flatly.

"What?" Felix said.

"Attach the Companion to what's left of my magic and give your power to me, then break the bond between us."

Felix shook his head. "You don't want my power. You hate magic."

"Yes, but I love you more than I hate magic, and it's

my duty to protect you. Let me do this."

Emya looked between them, feeling as though she was intruding on a personal moment. She had retrieved the Companion and Artyem turned and took it from her now.

"Can you connect it to me?" he asked, holding it close to his face, examining it.

"No, you must connect it yourself," Felix said. "If you can summon your magic. If there is enough left."

Artyem made a sour face. He did not like the idea of using his magic, even if he had just offered to take on so much of Felix's.

"I'm not sure I can," he said.

"You have to try," Emya said. "It's going to try to take all your magic. Don't let it."

Artyem took a deep breath and closed his eyes, holding the Companion in both hands. Suddenly, his eyes snapped open, his expression shocked, the Companion fell out of his fingers. Emya caught it. She knew she must have looked like that when she had first been ensnared.

Artyem fell to his knees and sat motionless, his head in his hands.

"Are you alright?" Emya asked, kneeling next to him and putting a hand on his shoulder. He didn't move.

"Finish it," Artyem whispered through gritted teeth. Felix picked up the bond breaker, but he didn't use it right away.

"Not yet," Felix said. "My power is still too strong."

Emya watched helplessly as Felix grew weaker and weaker.

"Okay." Felix went to hold up the bond breaker, but it slipped from his finger. Emya picked it up and placed it in his hands, but they were pale and lifeless.

"Felix!" she said. "You have to break it now! Felix!"

His gaunt features did not respond. Emya cradled his head in her lap and stroked his hair.

"Open your eyes, Felix," she whispered, hot tears dripping down her cheeks. "We're so close to being free. So close."

Felix's eyes flickered open. Emya placed the bond breaker in his hand. In barely a whisper, he spoke the ancient language. He slumped back as Artyem straitened up.

"Are you free?" Emya asked Artyem.

"I think so," he said. "Is Felix okay?"

"He's barely breathing," she said.

Artyem scooped him into his arms and lifted him. "Let's get out of here. Take the objects."

Emya found the Companion under the table, gathered the bond breaker, and stuffed them both in Felix's pack as she followed Artyem out. They practically ran through the fortress to the large front doors. Emya wondered what Artyem's plan was. They certainly couldn't run all the way out of the Twisted Realm.

Artyem kicked one of the doors open. They were

just outside the fortress gate when a huge shadow rose before them.

"You must be Azo," Artyem said as the shadow materialized into a man.

"Indeed," Azo said in a level voice. "And now that you are free of the object, you can give it to me. No need to fight. I promise I won't emerge from this realm ever again."

"My sincerest apologies, but I don't believe you," Artyem said.

"Well," Azo said. "If you don't hand them over willingly, I shall take them by force."

Artyem placed Felix on the ground and stepped over him, drawing two blades. Azo let out a long sigh.

"Very well," Azo said.

The shadow threw a mass of crackling light at Artyem, who slashed through it with his blade. Azo fought so fiercely that Emya could hardly bear to watch, but Artyem held his own, his blades flying fast and deadly. He slashed at Azo and caught him on the arm. Azo screamed and blasted fire at Artyem, but missed and caught Emya. She screamed as pain worse than she had ever felt enveloped her. Her magic flew to her fingertips and she doused herself with water. Incensed, Emya joined the fight, blasting Fire at Azo while Artyem slashed and dodged, occasionally slipping under Azo's guard and stabbing him, but the injuries didn't seem to slow Azo. Emya's fire seared his flesh as well as hers, but Azo only laughed as his skin burned off of him. Emya was getting tired, and slower. Artyem kept up his assault, but his blows became fewer. Emya had taken to guarding Felix when a spell hit Artyem, knocking him to the ground. He lay motionless in a heap. Azo advanced on Emya and Felix's prone form. Emya summoned a handful of crackling magic and lobbed it at Azo. It hit him and rippled over him, but didn't slow him down.

"Give me the object," Azo said, holding out his hand.

"Take it," Emya challenged.

Azo lunged and grabbed her by the hair. She screamed as she felt part of it tear out when he whipped her around and yanked Felix's pack off her back. Anger surged through her. Anger from being pushed around all her life. From Kamala bullying her and the Kings lying to her. From the death of her parents and being held captive by the Companion.

Azo pushed her away, but when he was slightly distracted by the pack, Emya spun on the spot and lunged at him, summoning the fiercest magic she could. It burned her hands and arms as she wielded it. She lunged at Azo, who looked at her with surprise and, for the first time, fear. With a crackling thump, her hand planted onto his chest, directly over his heart. With a scream of rage, she blasted as much magical energy into him as she could, willing every fiber of her being into the effort. Another scream joined hers, one of fear and immense pain. The power stopped all at once and she collapsed.

~~*~*~*~*

Emya thought she was dying. Pain pulsed throughout her. She just wanted it to end. Instead, her eyes flickered open, someone was crouched over her. From the texture of the clothes, she knew it must have been Artyem.

"Azo?" she rasped. Her throat was parched and her mouth tasted of dirt.

"Dead," Artyem said. "Or as dead as he can be."

Emya tried to sit up, but her arms seared with pain. "I'm dying."

"No, but you're gravely injured. I don't think magic will heal you."

"Felix?"

"I'm here," he said.

Emya turned her head but she couldn't see him.

"Let's get moving," Felix said. "She's not going to get any better."

Wordlessly, Artyem hefted Emya in his arms. She closed her eyes and tried not to think about how each step sent pain shooting through her. She felt Felix's hand rest gently on her shoulder, then heat enveloped her. They must have passed into the Twisted Realm. Artyem stopped and Emya was grateful for the moment's respite.

"What is this?" Artyem murmured.

"It wasn't here before. Wasn't this a desert?" Felix asked.

"They're vines."

Emya pried her eyes open. As she suspected, the vine creature she had escaped days before was before them now. She closed her eyes once more as Artyem and Felix started moving, though more slowly and carefully. After a few minutes, they stopped suddenly. She felt a sharp intake of breath from Artyem.

"What?" Felix breathed. "How did he get here?"

"I forgot all about him," Artyem said. "Even that he existed."

"As did I. Strange and powerful magic."

Emya opened her eyes and turned her head away from Artyem's chest to find a strange sight. Trapped within the vine was Prince Othilrin. His expression was twisted in pain and fear.

"We have to free him," Artyem said, carefully placing Emya in a pile of vines. Emya was too weak to protest.

Artyem pulled out his third and longest blade.

"If I cut the vines will he be alright?" he asked Felix.

"I hope so. He may be too deeply interconnected to the vine. Or it may kill him rather than let him go, but that might be better."

Without comment, Artyem sliced through the bottom of the vine below the prince's feet and above his head. He and Felix had to dig through the flesh of the vine to pull the prince free, but once he was out he sucked in a deep, ragged breath.

"Your Highness, are you alright? What happened?"

The prince coughed for several moments before he could answer. "I was taken from the keep by a shadow creature. A demon."

"We'll get you home, Your Highness."

The prince shook his head wearily.

"No. You must kill this monster." He gestured generally to the vines.

"I'm not sure that's a good idea," Felix said, looking around uneasily. "This is a powerfully magical creature. I'm not even sure how to kill it."

"Destroy it with fire," the prince insisted.

"Alright," Felix said, almost hypnotically. "As soon as we are out."

"Now!"

Artyem and Felix exchanged dazed looks.

"I can summon the fire, but I don't have to strength to summon a shield as well."

"I can set it aflame," Artyem said. "You make the shield."

Artyem and Felix pushed the vines aside and carefully laid the prince next to Emya. Felix created a shield around them while Artyem lit a flame. The vines caught fire easily and began to burn quickly. Artyem stepped into the protective magic.

An unworldly howl rose above the roar of the

fire. Though it could have been an agonized cry, Emya couldn't help but think it sounded happy.

The fire burned out quickly and they were left once more in the desert. Artyem picked her up again, and he and Felix supported the prince between them.

The trek back through the Twisted Realm was just as difficult as their way in. They stayed with the gray people until Felix was back to full strength and Emya was well enough to walk on her own. Her injuries would not heal easily. From the tips of her fingers to the back of her shoulders, she was covered in angry red welts and jagged scars. Felix had gently explained to her that the way she had used magic had been so out of control that she had hurt herself, though she was lucky that most of the damage had been directed at Azo. She would have the scars for the rest of her life. That was the danger of using magic with pure emotion. Emya had never cared much for her appearance, and she already had a few scars from her hard life on the plateau, but now she felt shame every time Felix checked on her injuries. But when he'd asked her what the matter was, and she'd told him she didn't like how ugly her arms looked, Felix just smiled and told her that he didn't care what she looked like, and no one who mattered would care either.

The prince was very interested in the gray people

196

and spent a lot of his time with them, attempting to communicate. He wasn't badly injured, thankfully, though he didn't want to talk about what had happened.

When they finally left the Gray Village, the prince was telling Felix how he hoped to create a communication system with its people, maybe even bring some of the people back as emissaries. Felix didn't think that was a good idea, as the gray people might not be able to live outside the Twisted Realm.

The Infernal Keepers were very distressed by the prince's story. It was their job to watch for demons coming out of the realm, but for one to take a powerful prince out of their domain was unprecedented. The Keepers sent a guard along with them back to the capital where the palace guard took over once they remembered who the prince was.

Artyem wanted to take up the prince's offer to stay in the palace, but Felix and Emya wanted to go home to Civim. There was no magic arch to take them home in that kingdom. Instead, the Prince ordered a carriage to take them on the week-long journey to a small kingdom that had its own transportation arch carefully guarded by mages, some of whom had come from Civim.

"What's the matter?" Emya asked Felix as they followed the mages to the arch. He had a slightly disturbed look on his face.

"The whole country, the keeps, everyone forgot about the prince," he said. "That's impossible. No magic has ever existed that could do that."

"The old sorcerers were incredibly powerful," Artyem said. "Who knows what they were capable of."

"Not that, I'm certain," Felix said. He took Emya's hand as he reached the arch, rubbing his thumb gently over her scars. He had been doing sweet little things that sent shivers up her spine, but this time he didn't seem to realize he was doing it, distracted as he was.

White light rained down over them, and when it subsided, they were once again among the Majesty of the Tritium peaks. The dim light of early morning was a stark difference from the mid-afternoon they had just left. The Citadel was almost deserted as they made their way to the eighth ring where Felix's house was. There they ate and rested for the whole morning. Then Artyem left, saying there was someone he needed to go visit.

"His friends in the guard?" Emya asked as she and Felix took a seat on the comfortable couch in the parlor.

"I'm sure he'll go see them too," Felix said, wrapping his arm around her and pulling her close. "But I think he is going to see his mother."

Emya was glad Artyem still had a mother who loved him. She couldn't imagine what it had been like for either of them after the death of his father, but at least she didn't blame him. She hadn't thought much about her parents since she found out what had happened to them. All of that seemed like a far-away dream. Her life was so different now, and she knew her mother and father would be proud of her. They only ever wanted to protect her. Now she could protect herself. And Felix was there to protect her too.

About mid-day Felix said, "I think we should go see the Masters now."

"Do we have to?" Emya was the most comfortable she had ever been and she didn't want to leave his warmth and touch.

"I think-"

A loud knock at the door interrupted him. He didn't have a chance to respond before the door flew open and in strode Evris. Emya jumped up with a cry of joy and ran into her arms.

"You're back!" Evris cried. "You're safe! I thought you were dead."

It was a long while before both girls settled down. Emya had to assure Evris repeatedly that she was alright, though it was hard to calm her friend down when Evris noticed the raw, red scars Emya still had up and down her arms. Eventually, they all sat down on the couch and Emya recounted the whole tale as well as she could to Evris, who listened with rapt attention. Felix and Emya had decided there wasn't a reason not to tell Evris, as long as she promised not to tell anyone else. Emya was sure she could trust her friend.

"Incredible," Evris said once Emya finished. "I don't know how you did it. You must have tremendous courage."

"I had no choice," Emya said. "Courage or no."

"Well, I'm so glad you're back and safe. And free."

"Us as well," Felix said. "And Civim is safe."

Emya smiled at those words. A sense of peace that she had never felt overcame her. She was free and safe, and her life had possibilities she had never dreamed of. She looked out Felix's window to the little cobblestone street and the other houses of the eight-ring. Beyond them was the rest of Civim, her home. Then she looked at Felix, who smiled that smile. Her smile. He took her hand and squeezed it.

"I wish you had told me about your dreams before," Evris said wistfully. "I sometimes have strange dreams. Sometimes they come true, although my mother says I just have good intuition. It's usually something that can be anticipated, like the rain or a cart wheel breaking. But sometimes they are very strange and vivid. Why just the other night I had a very strange and vivid dream that almost seemed real."

"Oh?" said Emya curiously. Evris hadn't understood that Emya didn't have dreams of the future, but she decided not to correct her friend just then.

"I was swimming in the stars, in the sky. As if the night was a pond filled with stars. And I swam to one particularly bright star and it spoke to me."

"What did it say?" Felix asked. A strange countenance overcame Evris.

"It said 'Let me in.' And I said, 'Who are you?' And

it said, 'Let me in and I'll tell you.' Well, this was just a dream, so I said, 'You can come in. Who are you?' And it said, 'I am the Being of All Magic.' Then I woke up. Isn't that a strange dream?"

Emya's mouth fell open, but no words came out. All sound around her seemed to disappear as the memory of that howling, that joyful cry, seemed to fill the room.

BIO

As a young girl Amy enjoyed hearing the tales of Redwall and Harry Potter read to her by her mother every night. As a result, she brings her lifelong love of fantasy to life in her writing. With a degree in Molecular Biology she also has a love for science and science fiction. When she is not writing she is knitting, going to the beach, or spending time with her family.

Made in United States
Orlando, FL
12 August 2023

36021426R00124